# THE
# FLAMINGO
# DID
# IT

SOUTHERN
BEACH
MYSTERIES

# THE
# FLAMINGO
# DID
# IT

## KAY DEW SHOSTAK

*Kay Dew Shostak*

THE FLAMINGO DID IT

Copyright © 2023 by Kay Dew Shostak.

All rights reserved.

ISBN: 978-1-7350991-8-7

SOUTHERN FICTION: Cozy Mystery / Southern Mystery / Florida Mystery / Island Mystery / Empty Nest Mystery / Clean Mystery / Small Town Mystery

Text Layout and Cover Design by Roseanna White Designs

Cover Images from www.Shutterstock.com

Editing by Jessica Hatch of Hatch Editorial Services

Author photo by Susan Eason with www.EasonGallery.com

Published by August South Publishing. You may contact the publisher at:

AugustSouthPublisher@gmail.com

*In honor of Charles Dickens and North Florida's*
*Annual celebration in his memory,*
*Dickens on Centre.*
*Everyone is welcome to experience this fun weekend on Amelia Island,*
*but if you're stuck up north in the snow somewhere,*
*at least you can experience it in this book!*
*And, as always,*
*To our home-*
*Amelia Island and Fernandina Beach.*
*While Sophia Island and Sophia Beach are based on you, the characters and situations can only be found*
*in my imagination.*
*Oh, and in my books.*

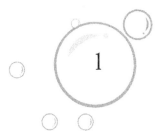

1

"Makes me want to tear all this jasmine right off your porch!" Lucy spits with a wave of her arm, threatening to spill the peppermint tea I just handed her.

"Please," I beg wearily. "Please do not tear down my jasmine. First of all, you'd probably electrocute yourself on the hundreds of lights embedded in them. And second and more importantly, I don't have the strength to argue with the Christmas Home Tour committee on what color we should paint the railing if it's exposed. Or what type of evergreen roping should be used. Or what shade of red or what fabric the garland should be. Or whatever they can come up with to plague my soul!"

Lucy grimaces at me. "I'm so sorry I got you into this, Jewel. I promise it wasn't ever like this in the past. It's that Jasmine woman that makes me hate all things jasmine."

Last March, when my friends and I wanted to know more about a girl who had been found murdered on our town's main beach, Lucy Fellows traded putting my house on the Sophia Island Christmas Home Tour for the needed information. It worked. In a surprise for us, however, the woman's husband was found to be the guilty party. Understandably, his sweet, pregnant wife moved away from the scene of the crime—Sophia Island—which also means she left the home tour committee. Problem is, she wasn't the only one.

One volunteer moved away when her husband got sick and needed care in another city. Then the committee chair left for Michigan to be near her daughter and her first grandchild. Then her two best friends, whom everyone said she'd strong-armed into being on the committee, quit too. In the summer there was even talk about the tour being canceled this year, but then a newcomer to the island stepped forward to save the day.

Jasmine Coffey volunteered her services. She informed everyone she'd overseen many large community events, including several home tours, in Rhode Island, where she lived before. She only moved to the island in April, but she seemed to be an answer to prayer. And I guess she *was* an answer, just not a very good one.

They say beggars can't be choosy. Well, we should've been a bit more choosy this time.

With a sigh, Lucy leans forward. "I can't complain too much because I was her champion. I knew I couldn't chair this *and* the Shrimp Festival. Besides, she seemed so qualified."

"Too qualified," I grumble under my breath. "Just ask her."

"Yeah…" Lucy sighs again as she picks up her tea, but then she looks around a bit as she settles back in her chair. "So you haven't found any more fake snakes? I have to admit I have a bit of anxiety sitting on your porch now."

"No, but the bulbs in the lamppost by the street were changed out for red the other night. I thought it was Craig with more over-the-top Christmas decorating, except we all know colored bulbs are absolutely not allowed on the tour. Not authentic,"

I say with a big eye roll. "Craig changed them back, but it's just one thing after another. It's fine, though. All the pranks have hardened me. I barely jump now at even one of those huge palmetto bugs. I just assume it's fake."

"Still no idea who's doing it?"

"Not a clue. It's weird. It seems so childish, but we don't have any kids around this neighborhood. Plus, what's the point? I even thought it might be about Eden and Aiden, either a disgruntled suitor or one of the wedding party having fun, but the pranks continued when they were on their honeymoon. Repairmen show up that we haven't called, folks come by wanting to look at furniture or livestock for sale, junk dealers want to take away the car or old appliance we're donating... Who in the world has time to make all those calls just for fun?" I throw my hands up and lean my head back. "I'm so over trying to figure it out. Hopefully they'll get tired of their stupid game soon."

We lift our cups, make a toast to that hope, and take a sip, savoring the warmth of the tea on a brisk day.

This weather is why people move to Florida. We're sitting on my front porch on the first day of December. It's midafternoon, the sky is a pretty, bright blue, and there's a light breeze ruffling the live oaks, causing the Spanish moss to sway. We have on light sweaters and jeans, but that's enough to keep us warm. The jasmine—the vines encasing our porch railing, not the woman making our lives miserable—is a glossy mass of dark green leaves. It will soon be loaded with tiny red bows. That's why Lucy is here. We've been tying bows all morning.

I wrap my tired fingers around my cup. The warmth feels good. "I love peppermint tea this time of year."

"It is good." She arches an eyebrow at me. "So… is it from the tea shop on Centre or a box from the grocery store?"

"If you don't know, why would I tell you?" We laugh, and it feels good to relax for a moment. I pat the cushion in my chair and turn ruefully to Lucy. "Our new porch furniture comes tomorrow."

"What?" she yelps. "Don't tell me…"

"Yep," I say gravely. "This old mishmash of castoffs left by Aunt Corabelle didn't cut it for the tour, but we couldn't afford new and I didn't *want* new furniture. I like this assortment of odds and ends. So, anyway, Jasmine's borrowing our home tour setup from some furniture store. We're storing all this in Ray's barn."

We share a smile thinking of our friend Ray's barn. Eden and Aiden's Thanksgiving wedding was perfect out at the barn. I can't wait to have a long visit with the new bride and talk about it all. "They got home from their honeymoon yesterday. I'm letting them get settled in, but I can't wait to hear all about it. We're going to miss her living here, but they're only a couple blocks away."

As a car pulls into the drive, Lucy clucks. "Break time's over. The boss is back."

I stand, drink my last sip of tea, and pick up the plastic grocery sack of tiny red bows. There are four more such bags, so we have our work cut out for us. Each red velvet ribbon is gathered by a red wire tie, like those used to close bags of bread. We're to wire the bows into the jasmine. The florist assigned to the Mantelle Mansion said it will look like a Christmas blanket lying over the porch railing.

"The porch does look nice with its new paint," Lucy says as she picks up a bag of bows.

"Yeah. Well, when Jasmine says jump…"

"Craig asks, 'How high?'" Lucy says, and we laugh as the boss, also known as my husband, Craig Mantelle, bounds out of his truck.

"There's not a white light left at the Walmart!" he proclaims. "I got them all! How's it going with the bows? I'd help you, but I've got to get to my meeting when I unload these. Only four days to go!" He hurries up the porch steps, his arms loaded with bags and boxes. I open the front door for him, and he quickly gives me a peck on the cheek as he dashes into the house, beaming. "Isn't this exciting?"

Lucy can barely contain her laughter. "And we thought he didn't like Sophia Island."

"Who knew he'd take to all this like a duck to water?" I reply. "I'm still in shock, but like my daughters keep saying when I try to complain, 'Isn't this what you wanted?'"

The front door is jerked open as he comes back out. "I'll leave the door open so you don't have to stop working to get it for me. Just a couple more loads." Craig rushes by us again and down the stairs.

The next time he goes flying by and then inside, Lucy sits down.

"This is going to take forever," she complains. "I don't mind hard work, but I do mind busy work. And I don't like not being in on the decision-making."

"Well…"

"I know. I'm the one who resigned. I'm the one who got everyone to threaten to resign. I'm the one who tried to call her bluff. I know. This is all my fault."

"Okay, I'm off," Craig says, coming back out on the porch. "You need anything before I leave?" He's wearing shorts, a long-sleeve T-shirt, and tennis shoes, his daily uniform now. He doesn't seem to miss his work clothes at all. In fact, he hasn't seemed to skip a beat from his sudden layoff, then retirement two months ago.

"Nope," I reply. "Thanks."

He tips his head at Lucy and gives me another quick kiss. Then he's bouncing down the stairs. On his way past the front of the porch, he waves. "I'll tell Jasmine you said hello!"

Yep. Craig is on the Sophia Island Christmas Home Tour committee. And he's Jasmine Coffey's right-hand man.

"So I guess I'm sorry for that, too," Lucy says after Craig has left and we are in a good rhythm with the bows. "I never really thought he'd go for being on the committee when I suggested it. Who knew he'd like it so much?"

"I certainly didn't. Then again, he was kind of at loose ends with his job ending so abruptly."

Before his retirement and since we'd moved to Florida, Craig had been splitting his time between his job site in the southern part of the state and up here on Sophia Island. September ended not only with Craig moving here full-time, but with our friend, policeman Charlie Greyson, admitting to accidentally killing his friend Bell Jackson. It was in an effort to keep drugs off the streets of Sophia Beach, but he also tried to wrongly hide his actions. He quickly made a plea deal and went off to serve his time, leasing his little cottage near our house to his deputy, Aiden Bryant, and his new bride, Eden. It was bittersweet to see Charlie take this fall, but there are some silver linings. I like having Eden close by, for instance. Especially since she's running our new event space business.

Eden moved out right before her

Thanksgiving wedding, but it was nice having her here all autumn as Craig and I were trying to get our relationship on a more solid footing. We're committed to making our marriage work, but it's not been easy. He was at loose ends for a few weeks, then as we started getting the house ready for the tour and Lucy was complaining about the new tour chair, Jasmine Coffey, he got involved. I guess it's probably been good for him, but he's such an "all-in" kind of guy and all the energy from his job is going into the home tour. I'm trying to not let it rub me the wrong way, but, well, I feel kind of resentful about how happy he is about it all.

Yes, I know that's childish. And yes, I know I should grow up and act better. But he's just so, uh, energetic and involved.

First with our spruce-up of the house and then with one of the other homes on the tour that is just down the street from ours. It's an old cottage that belongs to an elderly couple who were friends of his aunt's. As Craig has helped them prepare for the home tour, they've filled him in on a lot of his family history. Craig's family was always so aloof, and this is the first time he's had the opportunity to hang out and visit with someone from his past. The couple don't have any children, so they appreciate having someone look out for them.

As for the decorating, he always worked out of town and never took much interest in the holidays around our homes. Now, though, he has both our house and the one down the street looking like Santa-Land. No, wait, not Santa-Land. We are not allowed to reference any of that in our decorating. Not classy enough, we've been told. Everything is to be "authentic" to a Christmas in nineteenth-century England… or North Florida's approximation of it, anyway. Even the red in the bows we're working with is muted and matte. It's not candy-apple red. Not fire-engine red. It is "authentic" red. The evergreens are only pine or magnolia leaves, no cedar or fir. Our jasmine has escaped censure as it's alive—hence, "authentic."

I'd like to say all this isn't actually Lucy's fault—except that it is.

She—okay, all of us—badly misjudged her boyfriend, Davis Reynolds, but it's really messed Lucy up. He still hasn't forgiven her for dumping him after she found out he'd been hiring women from a local escort service. He's been bad-mouthing her to anyone who'll listen, and because Lucy's always had a sterling reputation, this whole thing has thrown her off. That's all we can come up with to explain her string of bad decisions, which resulted in her turning over complete control of the home tour to newcomer Jasmine Coffey. It was also her idea that Craig being on the committee would give us a window onto what's happening.

No one knew, though, that my husband would fall for Jasmine's spiel—hook, line, and sinker.

So, you see, my friend is right. It *is* all her fault.

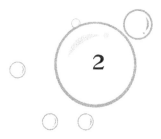

**2**

"It's almost like I'm the local person." Craig chuckles. "You know, because I grew up coming here every summer and my family was from here. Everybody else on the committee is new or hasn't been involved before. They all say it can be difficult to get involved on the island." He pauses in stirring the pasta and looks at me. "But I don't think we've had any trouble getting to know people, do you?"

"No. I think everyone's been really nice." I put a fork beside my plate at the kitchen table and turn back to him at the stove. "But you weren't all that sold on it when we first got here."

He shakes his head and takes the spoon out of the pot. "This is ready. I'll drain it if you can get the tomato sauce."

Once everything is on the table, we sit down. Our salad is fresh, but the pasta sauce comes from a jar. Neither of us are all that fond of cooking, but since Craig has moved back, we are having meals together. At least one a day, as prescribed by our therapist. Craig meets with him every other week, and then we meet together with him on the opposite weeks. At our couples therapy session last week, he said he thought we could reduce our sessions to once a month and then on an as-needed basis. The only advice of his we haven't followed is moving back into the same bedroom.

"Oops, almost forgot," Craig says, reaching for my hand and then closing his eyes. "Thank you for this meal and this day. Thank you for us being together. Amen."

I echo his amen. Our counselor is big on being grateful, and I guess saying grace does set a peaceful tone for a meal.

"Did you get a chance to talk to Eden?" Craig asks as he spears some lettuce on his fork. "I heard her ringtone a while ago."

"Just for a minute. She's coming over in the morning after her shift at Sophia

Coffee. She wants to see what the house looks like."

"I'll have the backyard done by then for her to see. I know it's not on the tour, but it'll give us an idea for doing the gardens once we open back up for events."

"I'm glad we closed up the event stuff for the winter. With Eden's wedding and now the tour, it would've been crazy." Picking up conversations, not just letting them drift away because it's easier, is a new tool I've learned. I'm working on applying it. "So you were saying you feel like a local on the tour committee?"

He smiles appreciatively. "Yeah. Of course there's Jasmine, who's brand new. There's also a couple of men who joined the committee with their wives, but none of them seem into it. They got recruited and are just going through the motions. They are all from somewhere in Ohio and stick together on everything. One lady lives near Jasmine, and they met walking dogs in their neighborhood, but she and her husband have only been here for about two years. They aren't sure they're staying, though. They miss their friends back in Ohio. Then the newest person is a woman named Marisol. She's very efficient. Just moved in somewhere downtown, one of the old houses I think. Apparently she bought a ticket for the tour and asked if they needed any help. She got recruited on the spot."

I laugh at Jasmine's recruiting fervor. "Maybe it's a good thing for the committee to be shaken up. I think, like in most small towns, the same people tend to run everything."

He doesn't look at me, but the way he shrugs and focuses on his plate, I'm pretty sure that's what is being said on the home tour committee. Especially by Jasmine. You can practically hear her saying it whenever she looks at Lucy.

"So," he continues, "this should be the last thing we cook until after the tour. I told Jasmine we'd already stopped cooking, but I figure spaghetti doesn't make too much of a smell. Good thing we have so many restaurants to go to, right?"

I set my fork down and goggle at him. "What? That's crazy. I mean, I understand not frying fish or cooking a bunch of broccoli, but no cooking at all? She can't mean that, right?"

"She says that's how all the home tours she's organized in the Northeast do it. Don't want the ribbons and the trees absorbing the smell. You know how stale things can get. It's all about the—"

"Illusion of authenticity," I repeat. I've only heard it a dozen times. "Yes. I get it. Luckily it doesn't break my heart to be told not to cook. I'll just be glad when it's all over. Then we can relax and enjoy the holidays."

He jumps on that, happily leaving the topic of the tour behind. "I hated that the kids couldn't come for Thanksgiving, but they'll be here in less than two weeks now."

One of our twin daughters, Sadie, along with our oldest grandchild, Carter, who turns two this month, caught the flu that was spreading around Chicagoland and had to cancel coming for Thanksgiving. That started a cascade of cancellations as the twins, Sadie and Erin—who lives in Saint Louis with her husband, Paul, and their daughter, Ellie—wanted to be here at the same time. Despite the fact that Ellie is only four months old, they wanted the cousins to get to spend time together. Then with the girls not coming, their brothers stayed at school in Wisconsin, preferring to come spend their winter break here. They'll all be here the weekend after the tour, and then the girls will be able to return to their homes with their children for when Santa comes. The boys will be stay until the first week of January; that's another reason I'm glad we decided to hold off on hosting events.

Goose bumps cover my arms at the thought of all us Mantelles together again, and I hug myself. "Oh, won't they be thrilled with all this?" We turn away from the kitchen table and look around us. Seeing our decorations go up step by step with all the hassle and stress makes it easy to overlook how completely magical our home looks now. Swags of red ribbon and pine boughs above the kitchen cabinets match the bows on the high-backed wooden chairs with woven seats we bought to replace the mismatched chairs Aunt Corabelle left us. In every tall window there is a single battery-operated candle (which is not authentic but the fire marshal frowns on authentic flames for the tour). A wreath hangs halfway up each window, with bows facing both inside and out.

Craig stands and holds out his hand to me. "Can I entice you to take a small tour, Mrs. Mantelle?"

"I'd love to," I say, accepting his hand.

"Maybe the maid will come and clear our dishes while we're away from the table." Hand in hand, we walk into the living room, and I can feel in my bones that Craig being here was a godsend. It's so much sweeter being able to share this wonderland—plus, there's no way I'd have had the patience to deal with all these extension cords and timers on my own.

There are three full-size live trees within sight when we step out of the kitchen, one beside the kitchen door and the focal point of the living room, one in the new window seat next to the front door, and the biggest one is situated in front of the side windows in the room farthest from us. That's a large open area we've used for dancing, like at Eden's engagement party, or for games when we do bridal and baby showers or for a small sit-down meal. When we're not hosting an event we move a couple chairs and lamps in there to keep it from feeling empty. The huge Christmas tree covered in white lights, bows, and angels fills up the emptiness. The angels are borrowed from some warehouse Jasmine has connections with. Despite being new to the area, she really does know her stuff when it comes to decorating homes and making everything look perfect. It seems sometimes the person who is most difficult to work with is that way because they demand perfection. And I guess when you're selling tickets advertising perfection, that's not exactly a bad thing.

Each of the trees are covered in strings of white lights. Once the tour is over I plan to add colored lights to the one here in the living room because it's where we'll put the kid's gifts. I believe children need colored lights, but that will have to wait until after the tour weekend.

We've taken down all our personal items and pictures. I already don't have many around due to the event business. I've never been one for a lot of knick-knacks or things out on shelves, so I don't mind them being put away. I have added shelves to the upstairs bedrooms and hallway for our pictures and special items to sit on.

The fireplace mantel is lined with candles and magnolia leaves. I'd never seen magnolia leaves used at Christmas until we moved here. They are large and thick, with a dark, glossy green on top and then, on their undersides, a pretty copper color. The florist and decorator for our house was at first frustrated with all of Jasmine's limitations. I've heard there have been some real battles as she's not allowed the designers to have any say-so. They've never had so many rules and demands in years past, but I must say our designer eventually made it all work beautifully.

One of my favorite things is how in the afternoon, as the sun is beginning to set, the sky has the same creamy glow as the candles. It's hard to explain, but that's why I asked Craig to set all the timers to four o'clock. To me Christmas lights before dark are at their prettiest. Now it's dark outside, and every shiny window reflects the sparkle tenfold around us. Everywhere I look is magical, and I'm so glad I agreed to do this tour.

Now, ask me that again tomorrow when I get my to-do list updated—or this weekend when there won't be a still or quiet moment—and you'll get a different answer.

Craig pulls our hands up under his elbow and squeezes them, pulling me closer. We've taken to doing this little tour each night after dinner. The hand-holding is a new addition—but I kinda like it.

"So, Mrs. Mantelle, should we see if the maid did show up?"

I turn to him, untangle our arms, and wrap my hands around his neck. We kiss, and there's magic there too. We linger for a moment longer than usual, but then the doorbell rings.

We frown and pull apart. Craig steps to the door. "Maybe it's a late delivery? It is getting to be Amazon's busy time of year."

He pulls open the big, old door, and there stands a very attractive blonde. "Hello, Craig. Oh, look at your house! It's beautiful." She steps inside, and then, after a quick hesitation when she sees me, she strides over, hand stuck out to shake mine. "Oh, you must be Mrs. Mantelle! I'm Marisol Sanchez."

I shake her hand. "Oh, Marisol! From the home tour committee."

"Yes." She's polished, and her cream suit looks like it would fit better in an Atlanta corporate meeting than our living room, even as decked out as it currently is. "Craig, I tried calling you, but you didn't answer. Jasmine wants me to have the most up-to-date ticket sales for her first thing in the morning, and I think you have a folder she meant to give to me at the meeting today."

Craig nods. "They're back here; let me get the ones from today. I haven't even looked at them." He walks off towards his, uh, office and—okay—bedroom.

I face our guest. "So Craig says you're new in town?"

She plunges her hands into the pockets of her dress pants. The action pulls at the buttons of the tight, cream blazer, accentuating her perky bust. Her hair is full and long and lustrous. I'd say she's in her fifties, but her hair, makeup, and clothing make me feel like she's so much younger than me. "Yes," she says. "I jumped at the chance to retire early and move to the beach. I feel like I'm starting a whole new life. You're recent arrivals, too, I hear. How did you get to know people? I thought this committee would help, but everyone on it seems to have all the friends they need. And Jasmine…" She wrinkles her nose, and we both laugh.

"Yes, I know what you mean." Then the idea comes to me. "I know! You should come to lunch with me and some of my friends tomorrow. It's an informal group that gets together at a restaurant every

Wednesday. No agenda, no activities. We just eat and chat. I've met my best friends there. We're going to a new sushi place just off the island this week."

She surprises me by quickly agreeing. "Wonderful! Do I need to sign up or anything?"

"No, I don't think so." She's the first person I've invited. I'm not the inviting sort, so I'm not sure on the protocol. "I'll let Lucy know to count you in if you think you can come, and then I can even pick you up? We order at noon, so I'd need to pick you up at eleven thirty. It might be kind of early…"

She pauses and studies me for a bit, but then smiles. "No, it wouldn't be. Sure. Sure, that will be nice."

"What will be nice?" Craig asks as he comes back to the living room, the folder in tow.

"Your wife has invited me to lunch with her and some friends tomorrow."

Craig frowns. "Oh, okay." He shifts to look at me and smiles. "That is nice. Well, here's the file. It was just in with the stack Jasmine gave me. I'd forgotten all that I need to get done before tomorrow morning. Looks like a long night of paperwork."

Marisol laughs, and they share a look. "So much for being retired. I think we're working more now than when we were getting paid!" She lays a hand on my upper arm. "It's nice to be in meetings with another recently retired workaholic like your husband. We keep each other sane. Craig has my address if you're sure you don't mind picking me up for lunch."

"Not at all."

She turns and hurries to the door. "Enjoy your evening. I hope I didn't come too late. People here do seem to turn in rather early. Downtown was a ghost town as I drove through."

We follow her to the door, and Craig opens it for her. "No worries. We just finished dinner and were hoping a maid might show up."

"Aww, Craig, I knew it," Marisol teases. "You are a man who knows how to treat his lady—dinner together and then conjuring up a maid! Good night, Jewel. Wonderful to meet you."

"You too," I say and head to the kitchen while Craig follows her to the porch.

Well, she's a bit too put together for my friends is all I have to say about that.

But I did the neighborly thing and invited her, as weird as that felt.

Being with us for an hour surely won't kill her.

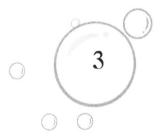

# 3

"There. That's the moment I really started crying." I point to the picture on Eden's tablet, which captures the moment Aiden spotted her coming down the aisle toward him. His eyes are wide and shiny. His lips are parted, and his hands are gripped together in a prayerful way at his chin.

"And then to see you on your father's arm…" I have to stop because I'm choked up again. Eden's dark red hair, as it's grown longer, has taken on more of the curl that her mother's mass of hair has. In the picture I'm focused on, there are springy tendrils all around her sweet face and a wreath of white flowers on her head. Long pieces of tulle fall from the flowers and floated around her but leave her face open. Her dress was a romantic Lady Guinevere style with an off-the-shoulder neckline; long, flowing sleeves; and a corseted waist. More tulle made up the skirt, and it trailed behind her as she passed us to stand beside her prince in his law enforcement dress blues.

There was a moment of levity as her father, the ultimate hippie, dressed in his finest Renaissance fair clothing, complete with a Robin Hood cap, walked her to the front. After hugging his daughter, he not only shook Aiden's hand but wrapped him up in a big hug. Then the big softie with the bright green cap choked back a sob as he made his way to his own lady Guinevere waiting at their seats. He completely forgot to say his one and only line, but Eden had only included the giving-away part because he wanted to say it so badly. As with her parent's choice of non-traditional attire, Eden let everyone do whatever they wanted to do.

She is wise beyond her years when it comes to choosing battles.

"How was your mountain honeymoon?" I ask as I get to the end of the pictures she has received from the wedding photographer so far.

She falls back on the couch, leaving me

holding her tablet. "Perfect. Just perfect. No airport hassle, no tours or schedules, so relaxing. I thought I wanted to go to a resort on some beach, but we live at the beach. I never would have thought of going up in the mountains when it's cold."

As I recall, a family friend of the Bryants offered their cabin up in North Georgia to the young couple. At first Eden was disappointed when Aiden jumped on the offer. He'd been to the cabin, and although he tried to convince her it was a luxury getaway, it wasn't until his sisters and sisters-in-law got involved that she got on board. They shared honeymoon stories of flight delays, exhausting trips with agendas like a cruise or an amusement park, or spending the week in the clothes they left the wedding in due to lost luggage. The ones who'd been to the cabin also verified Aiden's assessment of it being pure luxury.

"We were in the hot tub practically every morning for coffee and then again at night to enjoy the stars. We bundled up on the deck for an amazing view of the mountains, and the little towns around had all kinds of Christmas things going on. We ate so much good food and even had a couples massage at the cabin. I want to go back next fall, but earlier, when the leaves are changing." She sighs long and deep as she closes her eyes. "But I'm glad it's all done and we're back here." Her eyes pop open, and her voice dampens. "It is kinda sad living in Charlie's house. Has anyone heard how he's doing? I try not to ask Aiden about him because he really had a hard time believing his boss was going to jail. I'm not sure he's accepted it yet."

"I think everyone's kind of where you are," I say, "still finding it hard to believe and not wanting to talk about it. He doesn't want many visitors apparently. He says he just wants to do his time and put it all behind him. Fiona is flitting all around town acting like they had the perfect marriage."

I control my urge to roll my eyes. Fiona Greyson loved to 'cat around' on her husband, as Annie, my friend and Eden's mother-in-law, calls it. Fiona and Charlie are both from Sophia Island and married young. They never had children, and it looked like their marriage was coming to an end when Charlie moved out over the summer, purchasing the little house not far from here. It not being far from here was a bit of a problem when Craig was living in South Florida and our marriage was on the outs too. Thankfully, though, nothing ever came of our little attraction.

Hmm, now that's something to *really* be thankful for, though I don't think I'll say it out loud when we say grace over dinner tonight.

"Yeah, Mom says she's moaning and groaning to everyone who will listen. Which is a lot of people. She knows everybody." Then Eden leans up to me and whispers, "But she's also taking comfort from a couple of men she has no business being with."

I match her whisper, adding, "I've heard the same thing." I stand up as Craig strides down the back hall.

"Okay, I'm ready to show you," he says. He's already given Eden the inside-the-house tour, and she was appropriately wowed. The backyard decorating is all new. I've not even seen what he's done this morning.

As we follow him down the hall, he's already attempting to manage our expectations. "You understand it's not that impressive in the daylight. Luckily it's cloudy today, so y'all will get some of the effect."

Eden laughs. "Craig, I would never have imagined your Southern accent would come back so strong!"

He frowns. "What? This is how I've always talked."

"No, it's not," I say, "but let's not get into that. I want to see the backyard, and I have to leave soon." Craig grew up in Atlanta, but by the time he and I met at the University of Illinois, he'd lost all his 'y'all's' and drawl. However, after almost a year of living in Florida, let's just say it appears I've found myself a good ol' boy!

"Okay, just follow me."

He opens the door, but Eden and I both have trouble following him far. We're too busy looking to walk. Pathways of pine bark meander away from the small back porch, lined with strings of white lights along their borders at our feet. Strings of the same lights fill the trees. Planters of poinsettias now fill the yard with color. Wooden benches, the same dark brownish-red as the bark pathways, sit along the path and then, farther into the yard, in a couple of groupings.

Eden walks ahead of us as I pull on Craig's arm. "Where did you get these benches, the planters, and all the poinsettias? That all had to cost a fortune."

"Jasmine knew I was looking for stuff. Even though it's not on the tour, she worked out something with the ware-house folks. They brought the planters and benches when they brought our porch furniture this morning."

"So we just have it through the tour?"

He shrugs. "She said they don't need it until spring and can use the pictures for advertising. We'll also advertise for them on our flyers, just a little logo. And little signs like that." He points to a small sign on a stick that says 'Shore Wholesale Fur-niture.' "She worked with them on home tours up north, and they're trying to move into the Southern US market." He puts his hands on his hips and tilts his head at me. "They're good guys, and we're getting a deal. What's the problem?"

"No problem. No problem at all. I was just asking." I try not to bristle that any questioning of Jasmine appears to be crit-icism to Craig. "Listen, I'm going to have to go get ready for lunch."

"This is amazing!" Eden rushes back toward us from her quick tour around the backyard. "Completely expands what I wanted to do with events in the spring. We're going to be the hit of the island, I tell you. I'm going to take some pictures, and I'll come back later, closer to dark, to get some more. We'll start advertising this on the website. With heaters we can even open up this area in January and February." She hugs Craig. "You did good! Come look at this, and I'll tell you what I'm thinking." She hurries off toward one of the sitting areas with Craig at her heels.

"Bye, Eden. See you later," I say as I turn back to the house thinking about what I'm going to wear. Since I'm showing up with Marisol, I need to step up my game.

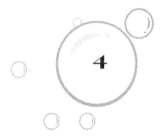

**4**

"Oh good! I was afraid I'd be overdressed. Seems I'm overdressed everywhere I go here. Thanks for picking me up."

Marisol was waiting on her front porch when I pulled up. She lives on the other side of Centre Street just one short block from the edge of downtown and one of our favorite restaurants, Café Mango. Her home is old like ours, but the houses are close together and sit almost on the street. There's a small garden area between the street and her porch. The light purple house looks updated, the porch welcoming. I remember this house going on the market, and I think it also has a state-of-the-art outdoor kitchen in back. Marisol has on a long, burgundy skirt, dark brown boots, and a soft, camel-colored sweater with a cowl neck. Her hair is piled up in a bun, high on her head.

My stepping-up game doesn't feel all that stepped-up after seeing her. I'm wearing tweed pants and a black shirt with black loafers, but this is dressier than I've been since Eden's wedding. "You'll find things are pretty casual on the island. Well, all of Florida, really, from what I hear." I put the car in reverse.

"Be careful backing up," Marisol advises. "This street can get busy this time of day, and the parked cars on both sides doesn't help." We both are looking backwards as she adds, "I'm from Miami but haven't lived there in years. I think my parents dressed pretty formal, but that may've been a cultural thing. They both came over from Cuba as children."

"Really? Do they still live in Miami?"

"No. They had me when they were already in their forties, so they've been gone a while now. I was an only child, so I don't have family there anymore. Well, I'm sure I have some relatives, but I haven't been back in a long time."

We drive away from Centre Street and up through her neighborhood. "I've never lived in a historic downtown area like this," she comments. "It's very interesting. Kind of noisy, but I'm getting used to it. Your area seems much quieter. Bigger lots and more trees."

"It's very quiet. We inherited the house from Craig's great-aunt, so we didn't look around at all. What made you choose to live downtown?"

She shrugs. "Just something new. So, tell me who I'll be meeting at lunch!" She turns in her seat, giving me her full attention.

"Do you know Lucy Fellows?"

"I think so. Petite, pretty, in charge of everything?"

I laugh. "That's her. She's our fearless leader. Then there's Annie Bryant. She's larger than life. Raised six kids here on the island after she was widowed. They are all still living here. Well, except for her youngest daughter, who is a television reporter in Jacksonville. So not too far away."

"Not like yours, right? Craig says they all live in the Midwest?"

"Yes. Twin girls, each with a husband and child, live in Chicago and Saint Louis. The boys are both at the University of Wisconsin. They're all coming the weekend after the house tour, and I can't wait."

We pause our conversation as we drive across the big bridge that takes us onto the mainland. Marisol stretches as she looks at the wide Sophia River underneath us. "I still can't believe I live on an island." She turns back to me as we hit the mainland. "So Lucy and Annie... how many more?"

"There can be over a dozen, but I think this will be a small week. Next week is our last lunch of the year, and apparently a lot of people come to it. After Lucy and Annie, I'm also close with Tamela Stout. She's a retired teacher. She and Hert moved here with their kids from Alabama a long time ago, but the kids are grown and don't live here anymore. She sometimes brings Charlotte Bellington, who is a longtime resident of the island. She's an original islander, I believe."

"Like the Bellington Manor Inn?"

"Exactly. Except that's her son and daughter-in-law and a sore spot with Charlotte. She can really be crotchety, so I wouldn't mention it," I say as we turn into the shopping center parking lot.

Marisol nods as if taking notes in her head. "Got it." She looks around. "So it's not far off the island at all. We haven't even passed the Lowe's yet."

"Nope. The Lowe's is just past here. This place, Happy Sushi, is new. None of us have been here." I cut the ignition and point out the front window. Cherry is walking along the sidewalk headed for the front door. "And there's the only one I haven't mentioned of my closer friends. The tall, dark-haired woman. That's Cherry Berry. Yep, official name, and she's a nurse. She and her husband moved here a few years ago from Atlanta, and one of their daughters has moved back in with them. Cherry works weekends at the hospital."

We open the car doors, and once we are walking toward the restaurant, I say, "That gives you a quick rundown of the ladies I know best. We usually sit at small tables instead of one big one so we can talk. We try to rotate so we sit with different people each week. With a small turnout, though, we may just be at one medium-size table. The ladies I told you about, with the exception of Charlotte, come almost every week. We try to not be cliquey, but you and I can sit together for sure. I won't leave you hanging out to dry."

She gives me an amused smile.

I don't believe Marisol Sanchez thinks

it's possible she could *ever* be left hanging out to dry.

"At least now I know why you were so dressed up for lunch. Ya coulda given the rest of us a heads-up. I felt like a boob wearing my jean capris and that long T-shirt with tennis shoes."

Annie gave me time to drop Marisol off and get home before she called. As usual I didn't get a chance to say hello, so I jump in when she takes a breath.

"Hi, Annie. I thought you looked fine."

"I did not," she grumps. "I was dressed for an afternoon of running around Walmart for the Shop with a Cop program. I usually help with the food shopping for the families. That's where I am now, waiting for my assigned officer to show up. I don't know anything about this Marisol. I can't believe you and she sat over at that table with Joan and her sister. They could talk the hind leg off a mule. I bet you don't know anything more about Marisol than you did when you got there."

"She's been to Minnesota, where Joan is from," I counter, "and she knows a lot about sushi."

Annie tsks. "You know that's not what I want to know. Does she know anybody here? Is she married? Why did she pick Sophia to retire to?"

"Yeah, that really *is* odd. Retiring to an island in Florida! Who could imagine?" I roam around the downstairs looking for Craig or Eden, but it appears I'm home alone. "Listen, I'm going to go. The house is quiet, and I have a bunch of shopping to do online. The kids are going to be here for Christmas next week, and I've bought practically nothing. I kept thinking I'd buy local stuff, but I haven't had a free moment in weeks."

"Okay. I see the officer I'm shopping with, so I've got to go anyway. Sitting here watching the hordes advance on the store has one good point: here *I'm* the one that looks overdressed!" She cackles, then adds, "Bye."

Before I sit down in the living room with my list and phone, I change my mind. With the afternoon sunshine, I bet the benches out back would be a wonderful change of scenery. If we're going to have a beautiful backyard, I should take advantage of it. I slip my shoes from lunch back on and juggle everything to get the back door open. A glass door back here would be nice to let more light in this back hall. I make a mental note to mention it to Craig as I pull the door open and step onto the little landing. I've not put a foot down on the top step before I stop.

There's not a single poinsettia flower left on any of the plants. The ground, though, is covered with bright spots of color that haven't even had time to wilt.

Our prankster has crossed the line this time. I'm calling the police.

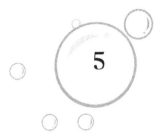

5

"There was only about an hour when no one was here, and it was the middle of the day," Craig explains from where he's squatted down, picking up the dead flowers. A policeman I don't know as well as Aiden has come and gone. He took our statements, took some pictures, and took a look at our camera feed from this morning. None of it helped very much.

Which Jasmine Coffey finds unacceptable.

"How can your cameras not cover your backyard? Who would know that? You say none of the pranks have caused real damage up to now. Why now?" The short, muscular woman is staring at me. Her spiked, gray hair bristles all on its own, but it looks even more bristly as she stares me down.

I sink onto the closest bench and proceed to pick up the flowers lying beside it. Maybe if I just don't look at her…

Craig stands, hands full, and walks toward Jasmine. "I have no idea. You're right, though. This is an escalation. We need to get the security company back out here. Before there was just overgrowth back here, so the only camera is on the door and around the corner, where we sometimes park."

"That makes it even more obvious this is someone you know. Any ideas, Jewel?"

She makes my name sound like she's stabbing me with it. She just doesn't like me, even after I've tried to be nice. Other people like me. "No," I whisper.

Sun filters through the hanging moss and low-hanging branches of the live oak trees. Soon the sun will be out of sight; it sets a little after five this time of year. It's already getting pretty chilly. Apparently that thing about your blood thinning is true. I used to never consider fifty degrees cold. I do now.

"I'm going inside." I walk past Jasmine without a word. Annie and Lucy might think that Southern thing of 'killing her with kindness' is a good idea. I think it's stupid. I just can't fake that I like this woman for one more minute. Much less for my husband's sake. He reaches for my arm as I pass, but I pull it away. "I'll go see about dinner."

Jasmine speaks up. "Craig, I need to reorder these to get here before the tour on Friday. I know this area isn't officially opened for the tour, but what if someone sees it like this? No, I'll take care of it."

She's very much the put-upon sacrificial lamb, and since I'm facing the house as I walk up the steps I allow myself a very big, much-deserved eye roll.

Jasmine continues squawking. "Since you can't cook here, come to my place, and we'll discuss the last-minute details. I texted the others, and they will meet us there. I'll have food delivered."

I have to admit that is nice of her to offer since we aren't allowed to cook, but as I begin to turn around and beg off her offer, she stomps across the yard, saying, "Jewel, I'm sure you'll be fine finding something to eat without your husband. From what I've heard you did just fine without him all these months, although you no longer have that policeman to keep you company. Craig, I can give you a ride." Her offer comes just as she turns the corner of our house.

I whip the rest of the way around to share with Craig a look of disbelief at her audacity, but my husband is almost to the corner, right behind her and telling me, "I don't know what time I'll be home, hon." He then yells from the side yard, "Don't worry about cleaning up the rest of the flowers! I'll get them later."

Jerking open the back door, practically pull it off its hinge and growl through clinched teeth. "No, go have your little dinner party. Just leave me here with the crazy prankster and a yard full of dead flowers." The door doesn't slam well on its own, so I yank it shut behind me. Hard.

Great. Now my arm hurts.

I get a text from Cherry after I get back inside the house, and I stop scavenging for something, anything, smelly to eat long enough to read it.

"I want to see your house," she says.

"How about now? Craig's out, and it's the perfect time of day," I respond.

"Be right there."

That makes me feel better. Craig is off with his little friends, and I have a friend of my own coming over. Besides, I don't actually want the house to smell bad, and I'm really not hungry.

Lucy has seen our house all along as we've decorated. Annie and Tamela are docents who will be helping with the tours as people go through the houses, so they have an official tour of all the homes tomorrow. That way they'll be ready for their duties Friday morning at ten when the tour opens. Cherry and I had said we'd find a time for her to see it, and it couldn't have worked out better.

I make sure all the lights are on and check there's a bottle of wine in the fridge. Okay, so I didn't just check—I poured myself a glass. I walk out the front door and down the steps just as she's pulling in the driveway.

"You didn't bring me a glass?" she says first thing.

"I didn't trust myself walking down the stairs holding two glasses. You'll have one soon enough. I just wanted to get a look at the house from out here."

Cherry is taking it all in. "This is beautiful. And you're right, the perfect time is dusk, when I can still see the house. Look at the candles all the way up in the very top windows! And the porch. That's the jasmine, right? It does looks like a blanket with all the lights. I'm guessing those are the bows you and Lucy were complaining about?"

"Complaining? I was complaining about *anything* this beautiful?" We laugh, and I shake my head. "That Jasmine woman is awful, but she sure knows what she's doing. Her efficiency has enthralled Craig. He's running around after her like a puppy with his tongue hanging out."

Cherry pulls back as we walk onto the porch and studies me. "Wait, are you jealous? I mean, after meeting Marisol today, I can see being jealous of her. But Jasmine Coffey? No way."

I push the front door open. "I'm not jealous of anyone. Just stating facts. Jasmine's very good at what she does, and Craig appreciates competency more than almost anything. He *is* an engineer, you know."

But Cherry's thoughts aren't on Craig or me or anything other than the holiday splendor spread before her. "Oh, Jewel, this is pure magic," she breathes.

She soaks it all in as I follow her around, letting the soft music fill the space and my thoughts fill my head.

Okay, I'm not jealous of Jasmine romantically, but Craig is used to working with accomplished women, engineers and planners and bosses. How could anyone not find that attractive? Appealing? I mean, all I've ever done is, well…

"Here, did you see the kitchen?" I bustle away from the large tree and my thoughts. "I want to figure out a way to leave those lights on top of the cabinets year-round. Aren't the kids going to love it all?"

She sighs and follows me. "Everyone is going to love it. I can't believe I'm working double shifts this weekend, but I'm filling in for parents with kids' Christmas pageants and events. I'd love to be able to go on the tours. Annie and Tamela are so lucky!"

"The hospital is lucky to have you. You're doing a good thing helping all the young parents out. And I overheard you at lunch talking about Jo working at the hospital? I knew she was volunteering, but it sounds like it's turned into more."

"Yes, yes, we can catch up," Cherry says, "but first, what about that wine I was promised?"

"That's why I led us into the kitchen." I offer her the glass and open the bottle. As I pour, she talks.

"You know I made Jo volunteer at the hospital so she could see the effects of those drugs she was so unconcerned about being in the community, thanks to that lunkheaded boyfriend of hers. And with her culinary background, she ended up helping in the cafeteria and talking to the nutritionists on staff. She's decided she wants to go back to school and get a degree in nutrition science. I truly had no idea what all was involved in that kind of a job. She's always done well in science and even thought about nursing at one time, so we'll see. Everything that happened has caused her to grow up a good bit." As we sit on the living room furniture, she stretches out her legs. "Oh, this is like being in a holiday magazine. I might not ever leave."

We listen for a moment to the instrumental Christmas music of Mannheim Steamroller. Then Cherry takes another sip and sits her glass down. "So, you and Craig? You know I was joking, right? I mean, you're not jealous. Are you?"

"Not jealous like that. But he's used to being surrounded by astoundingly bright, accomplished people. Men *and* women. I'm not like that. I've never really done *anything* professionally. I taught a little a million years ago, but other than that? Nothing. I don't even have interesting hobbies."

Cherry shakes her head at my words, but she doesn't act surprised at me babbling like this. I'm surprised. I'm kind of known for *not* babbling, but it feels good to get the words out of my head. I laugh and look around. "Like all this. If Craig hadn't been here, there's no way it would have looked like this. He's so efficient and decisive and organized! He gets things done while I'm dithering along, trying to decide what to fix for dinner!"

She smiles and shakes her head again, but then, as she leans toward me, her smile slides away and she freezes. "Did you hear that? Sounds like someone hit your back door."

I've already jumped up. There was a definite thud coming from the back hallway. "I did. Someone hit the back door or the back of the house." I head in that direction. "I haven't even told you what our prankster did today. I just hope they're back because I've had enough of their shenanigans." I jerk open the back door with Cherry right on my heels.

The backyard is completely dark, which is a problem. There should be at least the lantern fixture beside the door, not to mention the thousand or so little white lights that were on when I was out here just a while ago. I step down onto the porch just as the thought, *What is that smell?*, bolts through my mind. It's followed closely by, *What did I step in?*

"Is that dog poop?" Cherry asks. "Gross."

"Even more gross," I groan, "I stepped in it. Hold the door while I take off my shoe." I drop my soiled shoe on the porch. "I've got to call Craig. I can't believe they came back."

"What did they do earlier?" she asks, still huddled by the door.

I pull away from her and walk to the couch. "For the first time they did actual damage. Cut off the blooms of a bunch of poinsettia plants in the backyard. We called the police about that. And I was going to show you all the lights in the backyard. I bet we have a dozen or more strings of them all over back there. If they cut all those wires, Craig is going to be livid. Not to mention Jasmine. She as much as blamed me today. And here tonight I was home alone."

"I'm here," Cherry insists. "I heard something hit the back door too."

"Oh, that's right," I say with relief. "I have a witness. Where's my phone? I have to call Craig."

I pick my phone up and dial. He answers, and I jump right in. "You have to come home. They came back!"

"Are you all right?"

"Yes. Just come home." I hang up and lay my phone down.

Cherry picks it back up and holds it out to me. "You might want to call him back. Tell him not to use the back door. No need for anyone else to step in that."

I can't help but give her a snide smile and a little side-eye. "Well, depends on if Jasmine comes with him."

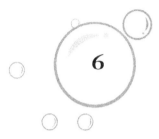

**6**

"Believe me, you're not the only one sick and tired of one Ms. Jasmine Coffey," Annie says as she collapses beside me on the bench outside the ice cream store. I'd evacuated the house while the docents did their tour this morning and told Annie I'd meet her here on the corner when she was through.

"Good! She's awful, isn't she?"

Annie stretches her face long, and her big, blue eyes roll as she thinks. I hear a 'but' coming. "Well, they may be sick and tired, but they also can't believe what all she's gotten done. No one's ever gotten all these stores to donate goods like she did. You did tell me your patio furniture and all that out back of your house is just on loan, right? For free?"

"Yeah. That's what Craig said. Apparently some company she's worked with up north wants to branch out into the South. That's all I know, but it does seem weird."

"You're not the only one with expensive, new stuff either." She looks around, then leans closer. "Shug Miller got a whole new living room set on loan because Jasmine said her furniture color wasn't authentic and clashed." One eyebrow slides up. "I've seen it, and she's not wrong. It's purple. Not mauve. Purple."

"But the new stuff looks nice?"

"Beautiful. Matter of fact, it might just get sold instead of taken back to the store after the tour. I wasn't interested, but if that dining room set at the Ponces' house is available, Ray would probably love it. He's been looking for a new one."

"Maybe that's the angle for the stores. I mean, there has to be an angle, right?"

"Usually is. Anyway, even though everything looks great, Jasmine Coffey's made the museum folks plenty mad on a lot of fronts. She's cut them out of all decision-making. Her costs are astronomical, but she keeps saying she'll make up for it in ticket sales. I don't think she realizes this isn't where she used to live. There's just not that many more tickets she can sell. This just isn't the same market as a big town up north. And after that poop incident at your place last night, she wants paid security for all the houses."

"Security? That sounds expensive. I mean, I'm the one who stepped in it, and I don't think it's a good way to spend money that should be going to charity. The police are sure it's kids anyway since they really haven't hurt anything. Kids have no idea how much poinsettias cost. It's just flowers to them. Aiden came over last night, and he thinks it's some teens he took into the station after one of the high school football games for drinking and some vandalizing. He wonders if they think Eden still lives at our place and they want to scare her to get back at him."

I've lost Annie's attention. She's staring straight ahead at the brightly decorated Fantastic Sweets shop window. "Want an ice cream?" she asks. "It smells too good to just sit here and not have some. Besides, I didn't have lunch. Come on."

I didn't have any lunch either, so I stand along with her.

She keeps talking as we cross the sidewalk and open the tall, old-fashioned door, made of a charming mix of glass, wood, and brass. "Aiden told me all that, too, and honestly, if it is those punks I hope they don't figure out where Aiden and Eden live. That house is more isolated, and she's alone there when he's on duty. Besides, kids will get bored eventually, don't you think?"

"*If* it's kids. It doesn't feel like kids to me. Luckily they didn't cut the wires for the lights in the backyard. Just unplugged them. One kid scoop of mocha brownie in a cup," I say to the young woman behind the counter; then to Annie, "It smells even better in here now." I point behind us, where they are pouring out choco-late-and-marshmallow fudge on a big marble slab. I get my cup of ice cream, pay, and move to watch the candymakers. In a minute Annie joins me, licking her cone of something white and creamy.

"I got the praline crunch. Well, you'll be glad to know Jasmine didn't get her way. No security."

"You mean someone said no to Queen Jasmine?" I grumble under my breath, "I'm sure it wasn't my husband."

"You're right about that! Craig ruffled a few feathers today, coming to her defense on every little thing. They tried to keep the squabbling away from all the docents, but you know me—if there's something interesting to hear, I'm gonna stick around. Craig definitely seems to think his friend Jasmine knows best. About everything." She pauses and concentrates on her cone. "They seemed *pretty* tight." Annie studiously licks her ice cream and avoids my open-mouthed gaze.

I can feel my eyebrows furrow and my mouth clamp into a straight line. Me and my ice cream are outta here!

I leave Annie behind to watch the fudge harden as I slide out the fancy door. The bench right out front is still open, but I take off, striding down the sidewalk. I apparently underestimated Annie's ability to move fast as she soon grabs my arm from behind.

"Hey! Are you mad at me?" She takes in my pinched expression and says, "You are!"

"I'm not mad," I insist. "Just, okay, what are you saying about Jasmine and Craig?"

She stares at me. "What? Jasmine and Craig? I'm just agreeing with you." She breaks eye contact as she licks the drips of her cone. "And well, you know, like I said, he is her biggest defender. You know what Lucy says…"

"Lucy is hardly one to listen to. She's the one that gave Jasmine Coffey the keys to Sophia Island on a silver platter *and* talked my husband into getting involved. Sure, now she regrets it, but this *is* all her fault."

Annie backs up a step, nodding strongly enough to shake her silver curls. "Exactly. Anyway, this will be over this weekend, right? And your kids will all be coming to town."

Looking into my cup of melting ice cream, I take a deep breath. I don't know why I got so heated so quickly. Just too much going on, I guess, but she's right. It'll all be over in a few days. I step to a garbage can and toss in my cup and spoon. "Yes, they will be here soon, and I can't wait. I'm also excited about Dickens on Centre weekend." I swirl around. "That's right, the bookstore! I wanted to buy a copy of *A Christmas Carol*. I bet they'll have one."

"Give me a minute to finish my ice cream so I can go in too. I've been wanting to look for the Joanne Fluke mystery set at

Christmas. It's part of her Hannah Swensen series. I hope they have it since it came out a couple years ago. She has so many it's taken me a while to catch up. I think this is number twenty."

"I just started on hers, so I'm even farther behind than you."

I take a seat on the built-in benches that wrap around the huge trees along the street and sidewalk, which are just outside The Bookstore, a delightful, two-story shop on Centre Street. For a Thursday morning the street is pretty busy, and I love the idea of shopping at Christmastime without a big coat. Or boots. Or gloves.

Annie sits beside me, giving me a nudge with her shoulder. "By the way, your house looks amazing. Best on the tour."

I smile at her; she's obviously trying to make amends for making me mad. Now I'm embarrassed. Why did I even get mad? It's just that Jasmine woman getting under my skin. "Thanks. I'm excited to see the rest of the houses. Can you believe I had to buy a ticket?" I laugh, and she joins me.

Two young moms with strollers walk slowly by as we watch. Then a group of older ladies shuffle past, two of them with walkers and all with shopping bags. They are laughing, and Annie and I share a grin. I should come over here and people-watch more often. It's really quite relaxing.

"Sooo, with the kids all coming in, how are you going to arrange things?" she asks. "I mean, with the bedrooms. I couldn't help but notice Craig is still sleeping downstairs."

Okay, I'm mad again. "What do you mean you couldn't help but notice? We left nothing, absolutely nothing, out to be seen!"

"Of course you didn't! But you know me. I looked in the downstairs bathroom cabinet. I mean"—she shrugs, pops the final bite of her cone in her mouth, then talks around it—"you'll need that bedroom for some of the kids, I'm thinking."

"Well, quit thinking about where my husband sleeps. That's my problem!"

Her smile is sudden—and huge. "Oh, so you think it's a problem too? I knew it! I told them all that's what was going on. I knew you were feeling good about you and him!"

"Told who?"

Her eyes pop wide, and her mouth

presses closed. Then she jumps up. "Come on. Let's find those books."

*See?* I think to myself as I trudge in the store after her. *This is why it was so much easier to not have friends.*

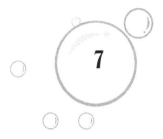

**7**

First there were little hoodlums in Halloween costumes crawling all over our backyard. Then my kids were little and running around my bedroom, asking where their dad was. Even though I couldn't smell it, I searched high and low for dog poop in all my dreams. All over the house, although the house was really more like a castle, a castle made of snow and ice. In addition, I'd set my alarm for six a.m. since we were told to have the house perfect and be ready to hand it over to a representative of the tour committee at eight a.m. sharp, so I checked my clock almost every half-hour to see if I'd overslept. (You'd think with a member of the committee living right here in my downstairs bedroom, I could hand it over to him, but no. He has to be at our elderly friend's cottage at eight a.m. for their handover.)

All that to say it was a very long and fractured night, and I *think* I'm awake—except there's a legion of flamingos wearing Santa Claus hats advancing on my house. I'm not sure they're advancing exactly. It may just be the fog making it look that way.

Fog? Flamingos? Santa hats? And yet I'm not dreaming. I am awake and standing at our front windows.

"What in the world is all that?" Craig says coming up behind me.

"Santa flamingos in the fog. This isn't something the committee arranged is it?"

"Yeah, right. No, Jasmine is going to have a heart attack."

I don't exactly smile, but I don't let him see my face either. He's right; she's going to flip her lid when she sees this. Tacky plastic flamingos.

And the red of the hats is absolutely not authentic.

My phone dings. It's Eden. "Call me," she texted.

"Eden might know something. I'm calling her," I say as I go to the kitchen to make a cup of coffee. When I came down the stairs, a quick glance outside showed me there was more to look at than the early morning fog. I remember getting fog last winter a few times when we first moved here. Something about the air and water temps colliding at the beach.

"Hey, what's up?" I say after she picks up.

"So the flamingos? That's your place?"

"Sure is. How did you know?"

"I'm at work, and a couple folks have come in talking about it. Is there a sign? Like, who sent them?"

"Sent them?" I place my cup under the coffeemaker and start it. "Who would send flamingos?"

"It's a fundraising thing. I was just looking it up. You do it, and then people donate to your cause to get them removed. Also people do it for a celebration. Anyway, there should be a sign saying who did it."

I yell into the other room. "Eden says there should be a sign saying who did it. That it may be a charity thing."

"Charity, my foot! It's those dang pranksters." Craig comes into the kitchen wearing pajama pants and a bright red Wisconsin Badgers T-shirt. "I've got to get them moved before Jasmine sees them. She's got enough on her mind." He starts his coffee brewing and then moves on through toward his room.

"Craig's all worried about what Jasmine will say." I lower my voice. "I personally don't care. I like them. I may keep a couple."

"I've got to get back to work, but if this is the prankster, then it's not kids," Eden says. "These things cost money. How many do you think there are?"

I move back to the front window and sit down. "Gosh, there's a couple hundred, I'd say. Seriously, they are everywhere, and with the fog they're really creepy."

"A couple hundred! I've not seen anywhere advertising you could get that many. That's over a hundred dollars. No way it's kids. Anyway, I've gotta go. Let me know what you hear. Oh, and take pictures for me!"

I hang up and settle in the window seat to drink my coffee. She's right. This isn't kids. But there should be a money trail, so maybe we're going to find out who's behind the pranks after all. Craig joins me, still in his pajama pants but with his coffee.

He sits down. "I've decided to just act surprised. I don't have time to pick up all of those things, and where would I put them? I'm going to finish my coffee, clean up what I need to here, and then go on down to the Ponces as planned. You do the same. We didn't have anything to do with the flamingos, so it's not our problem."

"You're not going to give Jasmine a heads-up?"

"Not yet. She's got enough to worry about, and this is really just out of our hands. Besides, folks may like it. Extra publicity."

"Oh! That's a thought. Maybe she did it. Annie was saying Jasmine needed to sell more tickets. This is the kind of thing that would get the Jacksonville news stations interested." I lift my phone. "Think I should have Annie give her daughter the reporter a call?"

Craig thinks, looking out on the scene before us. Our authentic Christmas Home Tour lawn is covered by the most inauthentic thing imaginable: bright pink, plastic flamingos with red-and-white Santa hats on.

"Sure," he decides. "Give her a call. But tell Annie to pass along the info without saying it's from us." He looks sideways at me and winks. "What Jasmine don't know, don't hurt!" We laugh and clink our coffee mugs in a toast. He stands up. "Now I've got to get dressed and get to the Ponces. You're doing the tour later, right? Let me know when you'll be at the Ponce house, and I'll walk through with you."

"Sounds good."

He walks away, and I think about how much easier this would all be if he was sleeping upstairs. No getting rid of all the evidence of a living, breathing person on this floor. That's one of Jasmine's requirements. The first floor must look as if no one lives here. Go ahead, roll your eyes; mine are tired from so much rolling. Maybe tonight we'll, I don't know… maybe…

Oh, look at the time! I've got to get dressed. Our houses committee rep will be here soon.

"I'd've thought the fog would be gone by now," I say as Craig and I walk onto the front porch. "Definitely chillier out here, and so damp! Look at the droplets in the Spanish moss." Weak sunlight filtering through the trees gets caught in the water droplets suspended in the gray moss, silvering it. A deep breath in gives me old sand, musty river water, and the spice of Craig's aftershave.

I place my hand on my husband's back as he walks ahead of me to the edge of the porch. He's dressed like he's headed to work—khakis and a starched, long-sleeve, button-down white shirt. All the committee members are wearing white shirts today to look official. The lanyard around his neck says that he's part of the Home Tour Committee, and I can tell he's excited. He's the kind of volunteer every organization covets.

With a smile, I step into him with more of a kiss than a usual 'goodbye, see you soon' peck. "Tell the Ponces I said hello. And hey, let's do something fun for dinner tonight." I swivel my eyes up to meet his. "Just us."

He wraps both arms around me. "I like that idea." Then a scream makes us tense up in each other's arms. It's not only very loud, but it's not stopping. We turn and see a woman standing at the end of our sidewalk, beside the smaller gate in our black iron fence. We both hurry down the stairs, careful because they are wet. Craig

has on his dress shoes, but I have on tennis shoes for a day of touring houses and
walking around town, so I keep up with
him.

We see the cause of the screaming at
the same time.

Jasmine Coffey lies on her back a
few yards inside the open gate. There's a
red-hatted flamingo nestled on her. Which
means the metal rod it should be standing on is plunged deep into her chest. And
even in the fog we can tell her shirt is not
supposed to that red.

Authentic or not.

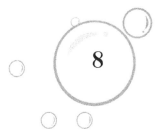

**8**

Craig bends down toward Jasmine, but I back away.

"Do something!" the woman, who is no longer screaming, demands.

Speaking firmly, Craig asks, "Norma, did you call 911?"

When he says her name I realize she's one of the women from the tour committee. The one who was coming to our house for the day. I move to stand next to her as she shakes her head and says, "No."

"I don't have my phone," I say.

Craig pulls his out of his pocket and hands it to me. "Here, Jewel."

I make the call and get things in motion, but the 911 operator is asking questions about the victim's condition. Craig stands and holds out his hand for the phone. As he talks he walks a little ways away, but I don't think he has to hide from Norma or me that he believes Jasmine Coffey is dead. We're still standing next to Jasmine in the mist and droplets from the trees when a police car roars up. Then another pulls in. Craig comes to stand next to me and Norma, putting arms around us both. Aiden is the second officer on the scene, and he hurries toward us, introducing us to the older officer who arrived first at the same time.

"These are the owners, Craig and Jewel Mantelle. Their house is on the tour today. Mr. and Mrs. Mantelle, this is Detective Ruiz."

"You found the body?" the first officer, Detective Ruiz, asks.

Craig reaches out to shake his hand. "No. This is Norma Krause, and she was coming here because of the tour. We came down from the porch when we heard her scream."

When Craig removes his arm, Norma moves to lean against the trunk of the closest tree. She's looking pale, and her pallor is accented in the misty morning light. Both policemen turn toward her, and Detective Ruiz says, "May we borrow a chair from your porch for Mrs. Krause? Officer Bryant, get the lady a chair."

I offer, "We could take her up to the porch," but the detective cuts me off.

"No," he says. "We need to stay here with the body."

Aiden has run up to the porch and is carrying one of the new white chairs we don't own. I cringe, seeing it being placed on the dirt, and then think, *Oh well, that's Jasmine's problem*, before I realize and shake my head.

She doesn't have problems anymore.

As the paramedics arrive, Craig and I move over to where Aiden has seated Mrs. Krause on the other side of the large tree trunk, facing away from the crime scene. The paramedics have given her a bottle of water, and she's looking better. Aiden is crouched in front of her, but he stands as the other officer comes forward and kneels down.

"Mrs. Krause, I'm Detective Ruiz. How are you feeling?"

Norma sniffs and then nods her head. "She's dead, isn't she?"

The officer looks over at the paramedics and then back up at her. "Yes, ma'am. I'm afraid so. Did you see anyone else around this morning?"

"No. I was enjoying the fog. Feels more like home. This isn't how winter is supposed to be in my mind. It just isn't right to be this warm. And then just as I started into the gate, there she was. Jasmine lying there with that bird stuck in her." She shudders. "Then I saw the blood"—a sob shakes her—"and all I could do was scream." She takes another sip of water and lets out a little yelp as another car pulls up. "There's my husband," she sputters before she dissolves into tears.

As he jogs toward us, the man says toward the officer, "Jim Krause. Norma, are you okay?" He bends to wrap himself around his wife as Officer Ruiz stands.

"Mr. and Mrs. Mantelle, what did you see this morning?" he asks as he walks toward us.

I blurt, "Nothing. Not until we came running down here because of the screaming."

"But you both knew Mrs. Coffey?"

I nod, and Craig says, "Yes. I'm on the tour committee. And our house is on the tour."

I look from Craig to the officer. "Jasmine is the chairperson of the Christmas Home Tour. I don't know why she was here."

He turns to look around us. "Where did the flamingos come from?"

"We don't know. Someone said there should be a sign saying who sent them. Sometimes they're done for charity."

Craig looks back and forth across our yard. "I don't see a sign. We've been having some issues with a prankster that have recently gotten out of hand. We actually filed a police report this week."

This gets us a very serious stare from Detective Ruiz. "Poinsettias destroyed, right?"

I'm impressed, and I smile at the new officer in town. "That's right. So you saw the report?"

"Something like that," he mumbles. Then, louder, he asks, "Why was Ms. Coffey here this early? Were you expecting her?"

"No," I say. "I mean, I wasn't. Craig was leaving to go to the house he's supposed to be overseeing for the tour."

Craig jerks. "Oh, the Ponces. I need to call them."

"Not yet," Officer Ruiz says. "In a minute. Continue, Mrs. Mantelle."

"But they're older and are going to be upset when Craig doesn't show up…" I trail off as the man's face doesn't move. He's got a strong, solid build and an angular, tan face, with brown eyes and dark hair. He seems very serious that we aren't moving from this spot till he gets our statement, so I keep talking. "Anyway. Craig was leaving, and I was just waiting for Norma to show up, and then I was going to be leaving too. Owners aren't allowed to be at home during the tours." I catch myself before I roll my eyes. I also make sure not to say anything derogatory about Jasmine's rules. It's hard to not say more, and I realize how much I've been complaining.

"Did you get along with Ms. Coffey?" he asks Craig—or so I think. Then he says my name.

"Me?" I reply. "Oh, well, I guess."

"Hardly!" Norma says from her seat. I guess she's feeling better.

Detective Ruiz's serious face cracks a small smile, and he gives me a very sly look, like he knows something.

What's that supposed to mean? I take

in a slow breath. "Well, she made things difficult. But I tolerated her fine."

We all wait for Norma to chime in again, but she doesn't.

"Thank you, Mr. and Mrs. Mantelle. We'll talk more later."

Craig steps forward as the detective turns away. "What about the tour? It raises a lot of money for charity."

Aiden speaks up. "I've been thinking. What if we cordon all this area off? Even the street. People can walk up the driveway instead of the sidewalk. It really is for a good cause and, well"—he steps closer and speaks in a low voice to his boss—"it would score you some real brownie points around town."

Detective Ruiz looks around and meets the eyes of all who are staring at him. "I guess keeping this under wraps is a moot point anyway, right?"

I chuckle. "Oh, you have no idea. Has he met your mom, Aiden?"

That gets me a frown and a sudden blush from the young man.

The detective sighs, then nods. "Good idea, Bryant. Sure. You know the community best, and if you and the Mantelles feel it's appropriate... But why don't we delay the opening of this house until, uh, noon?"

Craig and I share a look. We're the judges of what's appropriate on Sophia Island now? Craig swallows and gives Officer Ruiz a little nod. "I'll make a sign that the driveway gate will be opened at noon."

Both officers peel off as more first responders arrive. We walk over to talk to Norma and her husband, who is supposed to be going to watch over his own tour house. Craig talks to them, and I try to imagine what this will look like to the tour goers. The fog has mostly lifted, but it's still a gray day, and the air feels heavy. Maybe there aren't a couple hundred flamingos, but there are several dozen and not a sign claiming responsibility anywhere. And my feelings of them attacking wasn't imaginary. They aren't facing the street like you'd think they should be; they are facing the house. Every single one of them. That's weird. And not all of them have the Santa hats. Really about half of them do, and you know, even beyond that they aren't the same. Some are brighter pink; some have black-and-yellow beaks; some are all black. The eyes are different; some have two metal stakes, and others just have one.

Now that I'm really looking, it looks like we have a garage sale collection of flamingos on our yard.

Jasmine really wouldn't have liked that. I cringe, glad I didn't say that out loud. It's bad enough that I thought it with her lying just over there.

Craig comes over, puts his arm around me, and we walk back up to our porch. "Norma is going home to change into some dry clothes," he says. "Being out in that fog for so long, she feels damp. Then she says she'll be fine to come back and carry on at noon. Are you okay to stay here until she comes back? I'd hate to just leave the house empty."

"I think so." I peer over my shoulder; that's how long I feel okay looking at Jasmine's body. "Looks like they're putting a canopy with sides over Jasmine. That'll help prevent people from taking a look." I pause and put a hand on his arm. "Are we being cold, just going on with the tour? I don't know if I'm in shock or what, but nothing feels real."

He runs a hand through his hair. "It sounds so cliché, but it's what she would have wanted. She wasn't the most sentimental person; all business. Plus, well, I'd sure hate for all our hard work to go to waste. If we could help in any way… but I don't see how. Do you?" He grasps my upper arms. "Do you want to call it off? At least for our house? That would be no problem and totally understandable."

I chew on my bottom lip, thinking, but I can't imagine how not doing the tour would help. "Jasmine had no family here, right? Did she know anyone when she moved here?"

"Not a soul. Said she saw Sophia Island on a commercial and decided it was perfect for a new start. That's all. And she never talked about where she came from in a personal way. Lots of advice on doing a tour, as you know, but nothing personal."

I climb the first step of the porch, then turn back to him. "I say we should move forward. It's kind of her legacy."

"True. Let me call the Ponces. I'm surprised they haven't already called me." Walking a little away, I hear the moment when they pick up. Craig tells them he's been delayed but will be there soon. He listens, shaking his head at me with a bit of a grimace. "Yes. It is sad." He hangs up as he walks back toward me. "They already knew. That's why they hadn't called. Crazy how connected everything is here. So you're okay?"

I try to steady myself by drawing in a long, deep breath. "Yeah, I guess I'll have another cup of coffee. Good luck with the tour. I'm staying here until noon, so call if you need anything. I'll make the sign for the driveway gate and get it put up ASAP."

He turns to look back at the crime scene. "Thanks. I'd already forgotten about it. Hey, did you get the detective's first name?"

"No, I don't think so. Ruiz is his last name, though." I sigh. "He seems fine, but I can't help wishing it was Charlie we were dealing with." I watch my husband watch the new officer. "Why? Do you know him?"

"Don't think so. Just wondering." He turns back, then gives me a smile and a wave as he begins walking down the driveway, staying far away from the bustling crime scene.

I watch him until he's turned the far corner and gone past the side of our house. Then I hear Aiden calling my name.

"Here's your chair, Miss Jewel." He climbs the stairs with the pristine white chair and its green gingham cushion. "My mom is going crazy being stuck over at the Miller house, doing her tour thing. She can't believe she's missing the crime of the century. What do you think of the detective?"

"He's not Charlie, but he seems nice. How do you like him?"

"I like him. It's weird because I've known Charlie my whole life, so having a boss not familiar with the island and everyone is, well, weird. But he's got some really good instincts, I think, and like my wife would say, he has a good energy." He grins at the opportunity to say 'my wife.'

I grin back at him. "I agree. He does have a good energy." I quietly slide in, "So, what do you think happened to Jasmine?"

He just as quietly says, "I don't think she was killed here."

"Really?" I stare at the scene and all the pink birds. "But the flamingo's metal stick…?"

Now he's not looking at me at all, and he's speaking even more quietly. "The bird fell off the first time she was moved a bit. I don't think the stake was the murder weapon. Just there for effect."

"But the blood?"

He starts down the steps, turns around,

and lifts his hands. "That's all I can say, and that should be enough for you to tell Momma I was helpful. Right?"

"Sure. I'll let her know. You're a good son."

As I cross the porch and push open our front door, I step on the threshold, which causes me to pause. We had a cat once that loved to catch chipmunks and birds, kill them, and then leave them on our doorstep. I shudder and quickly close the door behind me.

Who killed Jasmine Coffey and left her on our doorstep?

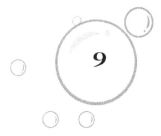

**9**

Peeking through the window seat's curtain to find out who's ringing the doorbell, I'm surprised to see Marisol Sanchez standing there. I hurry to open the door.

"I'm taking Norma's place here for the tour," she explains. "They let me in the gate."

"Come in. I wondered how Norma would feel about coming back here. It sure has been quiet. None of my friends are able to chat, and Craig's busy, so it's just been me and the silence. Well, except for everything out at the street." I catch myself bouncing on my toes and stop it, then wrap my arms around my waist to keep my hands from flying around as I'm talking. I need to calm down.

She bends to look out the window. "It

is quite a circus, isn't it? I was already at the Kieffners' house getting ready for the tour when we heard the news. Can I get a cup of coffee? They took Jasmine's instructions about cooking so seriously they took out their coffeemaker."

"But nothing smells better than coffee! I've had way too much this morning, I'm afraid. But I haven't cooked anything to eat," I say as I lead her into the kitchen. "Jasmine sure did have a lot of rules. Thinking about it, it's hard to imagine one person having such an impact and now being gone."

Marisol chooses her pod and starts the machine. "I know she rubbed you the wrong way, but that's so very understandable with all the rules and demands. How did she get along with everyone else? Not just about the tour, but in general?"

"I really don't know about anything other than the tour, but about the same, I'd imagine. You know, I don't even know where she lived. As for the tour I know the museum people weren't happy with the way she just took over. And she was spending a lot of money without plans on how she'd recoup it, except for selling more tickets. But, like Annie said, this isn't like where Jasmine came from, where there's a big market with lots of potential customers."

Marisol takes her cup and makes herself at home at the kitchen table, pushing out a chair for me to take. "Where did she come from?"

I debate having another cup of coffee, but I've already had two more than normal and I'm feeling a little jittery. Plus, am I talking too much? "I don't know where she's from. She just talked about doing tours in the northeast, on the coast, in the old towns there. I tended to stop listening when she started bragging and telling us how they did everything back there." I scoot the chair farther out and sit down, laughing. "Now listen to me! I sound like a native, complaining about the newcomers. I mean, I wouldn't do that, and my friends don't—exactly. Oh!" I start to stand again. "I'll have to open the gate soon."

"Sit. Take a minute. The young officer out there said he'd open it at noon. So you found her?"

"No. Norma Krause actually found her, but Craig and I got there soon after. It was just horrible. Who would do that? Listen, I went out a bit ago and got one of the flamingos like the one that was sitting on her." Looking around, I jump up. "Here, look at this." I hurry over to the cabinet above the refrigerator and stretch to pull the door open and yank out a grocery bag. "I don't think the police would mind, but just in case I hid it up here. Look, the stake on it is so flimsy. Some of the other ones have more sturdy stakes, but not this one. And it's adjustable so it pulls right out. I'm not sure there was even a stake on the one sitting on her because it was sitting right against her. I mean—" I gulp. It makes my stomach swirl to think of Jasmine being stabbed with a stake like the one I'm holding. Or maybe it's all that coffee. "I mean, at first I thought she'd been stabbed with the flamingo stake, but the way it fell off her, I don't think so."

"It fell off her?" Marisol has been very smooth, but her words leap out of her mouth and her voice is high. "I assumed she'd been stabbed with the stake also." Her thick eyebrows lower, and she licks her lips. "So you saw the flamingo fall off her and that—what?" She stops as I clap my hand to my mouth.

I slide my hand away and whisper, "I didn't see it. Someone told me. And he didn't say that it fell off her now that I think about it. It moved, though."

She leans back and lifts her coffee cup. "That's interesting. Do they think she was killed somewhere else?"

I know I'm talking too much, so I just nod.

"Really? Oh, that is interesting! I wonder why was she left here?" Her voice is lower now, and she's very seriously studying me.

Not saying anything for a bit has made me think straighter. Why is Marisol so interested? She just moved to town. Why did she join the committee? Did she have a history with Jasmine? Maybe I just gave information to the absolutely wrong person, but I've been here all morning with no one to talk to. Everyone is working on one tour or another—Lucy is even doing tours at a local church to coincide with the home tour. So many tours! And I have definitely had too much coffee. Why is Marisol so curious about what I know?

The doorbell rings, and I yelp. I'm saved! I have never been so glad to see a police officer on my porch.

"Detective Ruiz!" I yell as I pull open the door. "Come in!"

He takes a couple steps inside, and I put him between me and the kitchen. "Marisol Sanchez is here! She's in the kitchen." I'm still talking too much and too loud. My heart is racing from all the caffeine.

"Yes, they told me when I got back here just now."

Oh good. He's suspicious of her too. This may be the fastest I've ever solved a crime—and without any of the other ladies.

"What are you doing here?" he says as she comes out of the kitchen.

"I'm on the committee. I'm working in this house this afternoon." She's wearing a white button-down shirt, much like the one Craig is wearing, but instead of khakis, she's wearing a full, dark-green corduroy skirt. It has a wide, brown belt and deep pockets she's plunged her hands into as she walks toward us. She, uh, doesn't look like a murderer. In fact, she's smiling.

Wait—Detective Ruiz is smiling, too, as he says, "Of course you're working here this afternoon." He turns to me. "One thing you'll discover, Mrs. Mantelle: If there's a mystery anywhere around, that's where you'll find my wife."

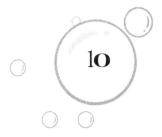

# 10

Detective Ruiz was soon followed by the first tour goers, and I saw from the line behind them that there would be no more time for conversation today. The docent assigned to our house bustled up the porch steps, huffing and puffing with tears in her eyes. She gave me a very leery look, which probably had nothing to do with another body showing up in my vicinity. Or possibly it had *everything* to do with that.

Marisol hands me my purse, keys, and phone, which were all lying on the kitchen table for my escape. Then she bends to whisper in my ear, "Get something to eat first thing. And no more coffee."

She whirls away from me, her skirt flaring out, and greets our visitors. Her husband—of course he's her husband—takes my elbow. "Let's go out the back door," the detective says. "Bryant parked your car up the street beyond the sawhorses blocking the road."

"So Marisol is your wife?" I ask as we march around the side of the house.

"Yep. Your car's right up there." He points past our house, up on the left. "You okay? I'd better get back."

Looking up as he walks away, I see the interest in me and the officer the people walking up our driveway have. I put my head down and hurry to my car. I'm glad I don't have to try and get out of our driveway with the steady crowd of people walking up. I'd hoped our house would be popular on the tour. Now I'm sure it is.

Drive-thru hamburger, a large bottle of water, and an ocean view. That's what I need. In that order.

My nerves have calmed down to the point that I'm not sure I could get out of this car if I wanted to. Downtown was a madhouse with all the visitors here for the tour. The merchants always make shopping in downtown Sophia Beach fun, but they really shine during special events. I got out of the historic area as quickly as possible, then made my run by the fast-food window and headed south on the island. As I drive down A1A toward the resorts, the beach houses get newer, bigger, and more secluded. Then, as I turn at a road just before the Ritz, there's a big public beach with a parking lot at the top. During the warmer months, this parking lot can be a madhouse in its own way. Peele's Point is often the first stop for partying students in Sophia Beach on spring break but also for young families who don't want to have to carry everything. This stretch of beach allows driving on it with four-wheel drive vehicles. This time of year it's more popular with folks who want to sit on the beach, walk a bit, and not get wet—yep, old folks. Like me.

Craig and I don't have a car with four-wheel drive, so we've never driven on the beach, but we like to sit in the parking lot, which is higher than the dunes, and watch the waves. From the parking lot it's a bit of a jaunt over wooden crosswalks to get to the water, but it's not too bad. There's a bathhouse and picnic shelters here at the top, so it's often busy even in the off-season, though it isn't today.

The fog has drifted away, leaving a damp, gray day behind. Nothing feels dry, and the sun remains hidden. With my window cracked I can hear the waves, and my eyes keep closing, staying closed longer each time they do.

I'm sure there's some kind of vagrancy law about sleeping in your car in this parking lot. Normally I'd worry about that.

But I know all the cops are at my house.

Sometimes you get just what you need, and I needed that nap. It was one of those naps where you fall off the edge of consciousness, but now I'm swimming upward and back to the real world. My eyelids are the only thing I move, and they only open a slit. There's still the waves, the seagulls, the breeze through the cracked window. Have the cars changed out? Have people moved around me? Driven past? Wondered about the woman sleeping in her car?

Call me a sold-out Floridian—I just don't care. And neither do they. My smile grows as I wake, pulling my shoulders up and into a full-on stretch. I'm stiff from being in the same position for so long. My phone is turned off and lies on the seat beside me. I've missed the rest of the tour for the day. Wonder what new catastrophe has happened this afternoon while I've slept here on the edge of the world. Annie, Lucy, and Tamela are done with their community-minded duties and are probably scouring the island for me, wanting all the details from the morning. It's good having friends—I'm honestly liking it—but sometimes these girls just want to know too much about every minute of my day. It's good to unplug and let them wonder for a couple hours. But Craig…

Slumping back again, I remember that, yes, I'm married, and yes, he's back in town. I don't want him to worry. There's a balance I'm having to relearn about living with someone I have a responsibility to. Someone who has the right to know if I'm okay—and I *want* him to know about that too. But without the buffer of the kids, it's a whole new balance. When we had the kids around, there was this constant checking-in on who was where and what was going on. What was the schedule, and who needed concern at that moment? Without that, how are we supposed to know when it's okay to check in or worry? When is it fine to just disappear? Probably never, right?

I turn on the car, then stretch to grab my phone. As I press the button to turn it on, I notice the clock on the dashboard. One twenty?

I was only asleep fifteen minutes? Shoot, I haven't been gone long enough to miss anything or to be missed. As I back out of my parking spot, one thing is for sure.

I've got to learn how to take longer naps.

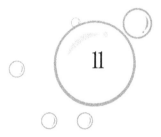

# 11

The sun breaks through as I'm walking up to the Ponces' cottage, and my sweater suddenly feels too warm. All morning at the house I'd been cold. So very cold. I'd pulled on a heavy sweater with my nice jeans and good tennis shoes. Then, with the arrival of Marisol, and then her husband, I didn't change.

"Honey, you're going to burn up in that," a lady walking up the sidewalk tells me. "All that fog was deceptive, but we're headed into the sixties this afternoon. Layering is the answer here." She holds out her hand. "Doris Goodwin."

"Oh, Jewel Mantelle. Yes, you're right about the layering."

"Mantelle? Oh! Well." She turns around, and the two women with her immediately follow suit. They walk close together, subliminally sending the message that there is safety in numbers—or maybe the message is more about closing ranks. Whatever it is, I get the message and stay well back of them.

Craig welcomes them to the Ponces' cottage, and I keep him at arm's length with a good stiff forearm. No need to give Doris and her flunkies any more to whisper about. Frowning, I ask quietly, "How have people been responding to you?" I peer down. "Although your last name is pretty small on your lanyard."

He nods. "Yeah, I noticed the whole Mantelle thing, and so I dropped introducing myself with both names. I'm Craig. Just Craig, no last name, no committee affiliation."

"Can we talk for a minute?" I ask.

"Sure. Let me tell Tamela."

"Oh." I lower my voice even further. "Tamela is here? Maybe I'll step outside and you can meet me out there. Promise her I'll talk to her later." I dart out the front door as he gives me a smirk and a small eye roll.

The Ponces' cottage is adorable. They've owned it for several decades, raised their daughter here while Mr. Ponce worked at the paper mill and Mrs. Ponce—well, I don't actually know what she did. I just know it was something she retired from many years ago. They are old-fashioned and haven't really offered their first names to me. Craig knows their names, but he also calls them Mr. and Mrs. The cottage is small, but they loved working in their gardens, so even though they get most of it done through hired lawn care now, they're the ones who laid it all out. It's delightful, especially in the spring and summer. I wander around the winding path and sit on an old concrete bench, where I can see Craig when he comes out of the house, but I'm tucked far under a tree enough that the visitors can't spot me immediately.

After a minute or two, Craig finds me and sits. "Whew, this is exhausting. How are you doing?"

"Better once I stopped drinking coffee and had something to eat. Plus I had a little snooze out at Peele's Point. So, do you know who Marisol's husband is?"

"Is it that detective?"

"Yes! Is that why you were studying him?"

"Maybe. Just something about him

rang a bell. All I could remember this morning was that his name is Daniel, and then his last name threw me. She's mentioned her husband but never said what he did."

"I didn't even realize she was married. As for their last names, she's a businesswoman, so maybe she kept her maiden name. Anyway, they are married. He showed up as I was leaving. She ended up working at our house."

"Yes, we did a bunch of switching around. That's how Tamela ended up here. So, has anything else happened with the whole Jasmine situation?"

"I don't really know. I did find out they don't think she was killed there and it wasn't done with the flamingo. At least that's what Aiden thought a couple hours ago. Who knows what they think now."

"Really?" He shudders. "I just kept imagining being stabbed with a flamingo, but it was just sitting on her chest. That's strange. Also, why would they bring her to our house? I can't figure out who would kill her here anyway. She doesn't know anyone."

"Except for the tour people. Sure makes me wish I'd been nicer to her."

He chuckles and pats my back. "You weren't that bad. She just rubbed you the wrong way."

"But I'm afraid when the police start looking for suspects, the list is going to be so short I might just make it."

"No, we'll make sure that doesn't happen." He tightens his arm around my shoulder, then uses his free hand to tip my chin up and gives me a kiss. Then he frees himself and stands up. "Listen, I'll trade places with Tamela so she can come out and visit with you. The house is so small I've heard her spiel a number of times and can give it by heart. Let's just get this afternoon behind us. How about we go off the island for dinner? Somewhere less likely to be talking about all this?"

"Perfect! Send Tamela out, and then I'm going to finish the other tour houses. Avoiding home for now will help keep my mind off things. I feel ready to even face Annie."

"Good. I'd feel better knowing you're around people." He walks back to the house, and I have a moment to catch my breath. Then Tamela is rushing at me down the brick path.

"Oh, Jewel!" she says. "Your poor thing!

I can't believe you found her. Did you really pull the flamingo out of her? Did Craig do CPR? We haven't had a chance to talk at all!"

"No." I pull a face. "Where did you hear that? She wasn't even killed there apparently."

Tamela has a sallow complexion and large, dark eyes. Her hair hangs on the sides of her face with dark bangs framing the top. Her eyes and mouth are matched circles that she slowly closes before patting my hand. "Hert says no one seriously thinks you had anything to do with it or they'd have taken you into custody. They wouldn't have allowed you to roam around just anywhere." Her husband, Hert, short for Herbert, always knows everything that's going on—whether it's accurate or not.

"Of course I had nothing to do with it," I say. "Craig was there with me all night."

"Really? Y'all have moved back into the same bedroom?" She grabs me in a hug. "Oh, I'm so happy for you both! I've always like him."

I sigh. "No, Tamela. In the house.

Someone did this and left her there. Maybe to make us look bad."

"Craig didn't have a problem with her," she points out. "You're the one that hated her."

"I didn't hate her. She was, ah, difficult. You know that. You talked about her too."

She pats my hand again. "Don't get so upset. Like I said, the police must not suspect you at all." Then she grips my hand. "Except…"

I look up to see what she's looking at. Two police officers are walking up the sidewalk, and they look like they mean business. They don't see us in their hurry to the front door, where I hear them ask for Craig.

We jump up and hurry to where they are standing on the small porch. I know both officers, but only slightly. I've seen them around with Aiden and Eden, and they are both around their ages. Probably younger.

One of the officers turns to see us walking up the couple steps. "Oh, Mrs. Mantelle. We were looking for you too. Can you come with us?"

"Where to?" I ask.

He looks around at everyone listening

and nods at the street. "Let's just go out to the car for a minute. Mr. Mantelle is coming."

Craig comes out of the house with the other officer. "Good. Jewel, you're still here. Tamela, can you handle the house, or should I close it for a bit?" There's a groan from the twenty or so people standing in line, waiting to get in.

Tamela shakes her head, her dark hair bouncing around. "No. I'll be fine. Maybe I'll call Hert to come over if that's okay."

Craig's smile is tight. "Sure. That'd be great." He holds the door for her and then comes out and down the porch steps. He takes my hand, and we follow the police officer I'd talked to. The other one follows behind us.

I ignore all the phones taking our picture. I was hot before, but now I'm dripping sweat.

At the car, parked mercifully in the shade, I lean against the hood; Craig stands ramrod straight beside me. Neither officer says anything; they are looking at one of their phones. Then one holds it out to us. "Here, it's Sergeant Johnson."

I groan. This man is not sharp or intuitive or even nice. How he became a detective was always a mystery to me. Then with Charlie's arrest he was apparently promoted because now he is Sergeant Johnson.

"Good," he shouts through the phone. "They found you both together. Makes it easier. Now, these two officers are going to be assigned to you until we get this case wrapped up. Men, don't let the Mantelles out of your sight."

All four of us are staring at the phone. It goes dark until the young man holding it pulls it toward him, looking at it closer. "Uh, he hung up. Yeah…"

A chill moves over me despite my sweater. "Is he arresting us? What does he mean that you're assigned to us?"

They look at each other, then look at us. The one with the phone answers, "Uh, don't think so. We, uh, were just told to come find you." He walks around the car toward the driver's side. "Let me make a call."

He gets in the car and closes the door, then talks too quietly for us to hear. But in just a moment he pops back out. "No. We're for your protection."

Craig puts an arm around me. "Protection! What's going on?"

Both officers shrug, and the one with

the phone asks, "So are we going back up to this house? Or somewhere else? Y'all don't have to stay together. I'll stay with you, Mr. Mantelle, and Ty will go with you, Mrs. Mantelle." He smiles as if everything is just great. "Just do whatever you were going to do. Ignore us."

Ty smiles at me, and suddenly it's obvious he's not as old as Aiden and Eden. He's a baby. "Have you…" I pause before I can ask him if he's graduated high school. "Have you ever done this before? What do we need protection from?"

"Sure!" he says, but I can tell from the way he looks away he's not being truthful. "Just a precaution, I'm sure."

"Okay, Ty. I just want to go home. Craig, you can stay here. I'll see you at home soon." I lean over to give him a hug and whisper, "I'll talk to Aiden and the detective at the house and call you."

"Sounds good. I think that's Hert pulling up. Be careful." He waves at Hert and heads him off from coming over to me and the officer. Hert likes to talk, and I want to get home and get some answers. I give Ty a smile and start walking to my car.

"Uh, ma'am?" I turn around. He's

smiling again. "Can you give me a ride? We just came in the one car."

"Sure. I'm down here."

Officer Ty Cartle, I learn on the short drive over to our house, has graduated from high school and even the police academy. He's from Jacksonville but loves the beach and likes his job here. He says Sophia Island decided to hire more officers from out of town recently. He doesn't know why exactly. I grimace and nod. I feel pretty sure *I* know why. Something to do with Officer Charlie Greyson being in prison. We pull up and try to edge past the line of people to pull into my driveway; however, before I get very far, Officer Cartle jumps out and displays everything he learned in Crowd Control 101. This is exactly what I didn't want, everyone knowing I'm driving around with a cop in the car.

I pull down the drive as far as I can, jump out of the car, and hurry to the back door, Ty on my heels. I knock, and Marisol opens the door before I can get my key in the lock.

"You're back," she says. "I saw you pulling in."

"Yeah, this is Officer Ty. I have to go

upstairs and change out of this sweater before I die of heat exhaustion," I say as I march past her, past the people watching, past the docent whom I don't know, and then past the sign saying the upstairs is off-limits. The air-conditioning in the house is on high, and it feels wonderful. The Christmas music plays, the candles are lit, and every light is twinkling for all it's worth. As I walk up the stairs, tears come to my eyes. Everything is just as we planned. Just as Jasmine planned. It's beautiful, and the woman responsible is dead.

I've had a nap. Now I need a good cry.

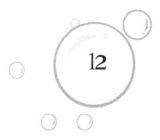

# 12

"Well, Tamela, you got to work with Craig today." Annie is blustery in her indignation. "That's why you were able to be on your phone. I had that mean tour committee woman from Iowa or Ohio or somewhere. I can't ever remember which it is, and she watched me with an eagle eye. Tried to act like she knew me. She even said"—here Annie takes on a high-pitched, snarky tone—"'I've been warned about you, Ms. Bryant, and I'll have no shenanigans on my watch.'"

That makes me giggle, but I bury it in the palm of my hand so I can listen a moment longer while hiding at the top of the stairs.

"Oh, that's priceless! She's heard about you and your shenanigans." Lucy laughs as she jerks Annie's chain. Then she yells, "Jewel, get down here. I can see the light from your bedroom door, so I know you're there in the hall." I look back and see she's right; light is pouring out my door as the sunlight comes through the live oak branches and moss.

"Okay, I'm coming." I groan a bit as I straighten up. "I was trying to wait until the tours finished. You must've cut your tours short, seeing as it's just barely after four o'clock."

A very long shower allowed me to get all my tears out. Then I took my time getting dressed and looking through local social media; I even took the time to call both of our daughters. I didn't mention the drama here, just said I was hiding out from the tours. Now I have on a pair of soft, old khakis, new boat shoes, and a long-sleeve, blue-and-white-striped shirt. I've let my hair grow out. It's currently slicked back in a low ponytail, and I took the time to put on some light makeup. After so many frantic weeks of getting everything ready for the tour, it was quite peaceful alone upstairs.

"Oh, honey," Annie says from where she waits at the bottom of the stairs. "You look as refreshed as I feel dragged through a cow pile. Give me a hug anyway."

"So who all is here?" I ask. "Hey, Lucy, Tamela. What about Craig?" I'd texted him before my shower to tell him the police were already gone so I couldn't ask them anything, and he'd told me to stay here and rest. Then I heard nothing more from him.

Marisol pokes her head out of the kitchen. "Craig called me. He'll be here soon."

Annie glares at Marisol, who laughs and turns back to the kitchen.

Annie quietly spits as she passes me, going back to her chair, "You need to put a stop to that right there. Whatever *it* is. I don't trust that woman. There's something going on!"

As I walk past Annie who has dropped into her seat, still indignant, I widen my eyes, nod, and then sit on the couch corner, leaning in. She bends toward me for the scoop. I whisper, "You're right. She's married to the police detective in charge of Jasmine's case."

Annie rears back, confusion all over her face, bright blue eyes blinking. "Her?" She turns to Lucy. "Did you know this?"

"I knew," Tamela says, raising her hand. "Hert knew."

Lucy shrugs. "I heard something today, but it didn't make sense. I mean, I even checked their names."

"They don't match," Marisol says loudly, coming from the kitchen with a tray. "A woman changing her name to her husband's is not a Hispanic tradition. I married Daniel when I already had my career in full gear, so it wasn't just the cultural aspects of me keeping my name that I liked. I am, however, very much married to Detective Daniel Ruiz and have been for seventeen years. We are enjoying Sophia Island and plan to make it our forever home. Nice to meet you all." She bows as she takes a seat. "Here are some cheese toasties, and Jewel, what can I get you to drink? The other ladies are having tea or water."

"You don't need to wait on me," I object, but she doesn't let me finish.

Instead, she confidently says, "I'm thinking a cup of hot tea *and* a glass of water. Sit back and relax."

Tamela is enjoying one of the little melted cheese squares, which I think is just white bread cut in pieces with a slice of cheese on top and toasted. That would fit with the lacking ingredients we have in the kitchen. She picks up another one before she's finished chewing the first one and says, "These remind me of being a kid on a winter morning. Maybe I should get a cup of hot chocolate."

Lucy shushes her. "Hurry, what else did Hert know about her?"

Tamela thinks and chews. "Well, you know Hert talks so much it's hard to listen. Yeah, I can't think of anything else."

Annie and Lucy share an eye roll, but I can't help but smile. They are all so predictable, and I'm so glad they are here. "Oh! Where's Officer Ty?" I look around.

"Here's your tea and water," Marisol says as she brings in the cup and saucer and glass. "Ty's outside on the porch. I made him some cheese toast also, and he did go for hot chocolate. He's really just a big boy." She returns to the kitchen, then comes back with her own cup and saucer. "Whew. What a day!" She sits on the couch down a bit from me.

Annie's head tilts. She pulls in a breath and then starts in on Marisol. "So you're married to my son's boss, I hear. Why didn't you say something when you had lunch with us?"

Marisol rolls her eyes. "You do remember who Jewel and I were seated with? It was hard to get a word in edgewise."

I mouth, "Joan and her sister."

The other three acknowledge the problem.

"But you're also right. I wanted to meet you on my own first." Marisol leans forward. "Daniel and I have never been big fish in a small pond. We both went from Miami to Charlotte. Not together, mind you. We had some shared acquaintances in Miami, but he moved there after some bad stuff in Miami with the police force. It's a difficult place to enforce the law, as you can imagine. Charlotte seemed much calmer, but it's still a pretty big town. I made my way there after college and working in South Florida a few years. I was in the financial industry, and Charlotte is a banking capitol. We met, dated a while, and then got married. Lately, though, Charlotte felt too big. We decided we were ready for a small town, to make friends and retire. Well, he'll retire eventually. I already did!" She sits back, holding her cup and saucer in her hands. Story complete.

Annie nods her approval of the information dump. "Okay, that does make sense. You're smart to realize you're in a small pond now. It will take some getting used to. Aiden likes your husband. But of course that was before I knew he was your husband." She squints at Marisol. "I wondered why a good-looking man like that would be single. This does make more sense."

Lucy slaps at her arm. "Annie!" Then she smiles and adds, "But he is good-looking. I'm sad to hear he's off the market."

"Lucy's recently on the market," Tamela explains, and Lucy actually does slap her on the arm.

"I am *not* on the market! Anyway. What's the story with Officer Ty as y'all keep calling him?"

I draw in a deep breath. "Protection? That's all I know. I imagine Craig is at the police station now trying to find out what's going on."

"Well," Marisol says excitedly as she sets her tea down and leans forward again. "Jasmine's condo was a wreck. Torn completely up, which suggests the murderer was looking for something. They still don't know where she was killed. No blood here or at her condo like there should be with that injury." She pauses and looks around the group until she's facing only me. "With her being left here, I think Daniel is just being cautious."

"Oh, so it's not like y'all are under house arrest?" Tamela says as she scrolls on her phone. "I mean, that's what everyone thinks."

"Who's everyone?" I ask, but I can see by the way Annie and Lucy aren't looking at me that they might've thought that too.

I groan. "That's just great."

"Want me to let Hert know the truth? He's all over the island's social media pages." Tamela sits with her phone at the ready.

Annie scowls. "I don't think so. If the murderer thinks the police suspect Jewel and Craig, then maybe they'll be more apt to make a mistake. I think that's why she was left here. To make y'all look guilty."

"I agree," Marisol says eagerly. "That's good thinking, Annie."

Annie beams and puffs up. Like she ever needs a reason to puff up.

Marisol continues, "And Hert being good at social media will definitely come in handy. That's so good to know!"

Now Tamela's beaming.

Lucy cocks an eyebrow at me and motions at Marisol with a tip of her head to say she's not so easily swayed. But then…

"Did you know when we told people in Charlotte we were moving to Sophia Island, Lucy, your name came up several times? Apparently your classes on tourism and city involvement at the chamber of commerce conferences are in high demand. You've made quite a name for Sophia Island in the Charlotte area."

Lucy squirms, licking her lips as if trying to tamp down her chamber of commerce smile. "My classes *are* well received, and Charlotte is a lovely and gracious town."

"So, Marisol, want to tell them your little secret?" I ask, but I don't give her time to answer. "I found out from her husband's own lips that his wife is addicted to mysteries. And… she has heard about our little group's string of successful cases."

Now they really love her! My friends' eyes shine so brightly that they challenge the Christmas tree lights. "You heard about us? How? From who?" They are all on the edge of their seats, all talking at once, and the stars in their eyes are also circling their heads.

Marisol looks at me, then at the others, waiting for things to quiet. "Charlie Greyson. Daniel had met him a couple times. They really hit it off, and Charlie was actually on the lookout for a new position for Daniel in a small town in Florida. Like I mentioned, we were ready for that, and we also wanted to be back in Florida. Not South Florida, but still close to the beach, the nice weather, you know." She sighs. "Charlie, of course, never thought it would be Sophia Island."

That slows everyone down. It's been hard knowing we had a hand in everything coming out, but we also knew it had to, even if it meant Charlie going to jail. I'd never imagined he and Daniel would be friends, and I'm as surprised as the others. But it also makes perfect sense. Charlie took care of his island, and his friends, even as he paid the price.

Annie rubs her hand on her thigh. "I guess I always knew Charlie couldn't come back to the police force here; I mean, he'll be ready to retire when he gets out. I wonder if Aiden knows he and Daniel know each other?"

"Oh," Marisol says with a jerk of her head. "No, no one at the station can know. Charlie doesn't want to taint Daniel's reputation, and there are still some really hard feelings toward, and suspicions of, Charlie there."

Lucy nods. "Very true. Okay, we'll only tell Cherry. You met her at lunch, right? She's part of our group. It will make her feel better too." She turns to our friend, whose phone is still at the ready. "And Tamela…"

"I know," she says. "I can't tell Hert. He'd never be able to keep this quiet. Don't worry. I'm going to put it right out of my mind this minute."

Marisol looks worried, but I pat her leg. "She won't say anything. She knows her husband better than anyone. He might guess something like this, though. He is pretty intuitive. But in our favor, he's so often wrong that no one will listen to him if he does put it out as a thought."

Tamela reaches down to her purse, which is on the floor, and pulls out her notebook. "I'm ready to get to work. Come on, ladies. Charlie—and Detective Ruiz—believe in us!"

We all laugh, but I can see Marisol bite

her lip as she realizes she might've created a monster. Oh well.

Too late now.

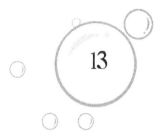

# 13

"Detective Ruiz knows Charlie Greyson," Craig says as we drive out across the bridge connecting Sophia to the mainland.

"He told you? I thought he might." I shift in the passenger seat to look at my husband. He looks tired. My friends and I hadn't gotten very far in our investigations when he got home. I was right that he had gone to the police station.

He chuckles. "I think that was partway behind our protection this afternoon. He's afraid something will happen to one of Charlie's people on his watch. I've gotta say, I do like that he's having someone watch the house all the time. I'm not sure the prankster is the one who killed Jasmine, but I'm afraid they might be using them for cover or to at least confuse things."

"That's what we came up with too." I check the rearview mirror and add, "I notice there are no police cars following us."

"It was decided as long as we were together we'd be okay, especially since I told him we were going off island. He seems like a decent guy. It does make me feel better that he knew Charlie. I actually at one point today wondered if he or Marisol came here for Jasmine."

"Me too! I mean, it has to be someone from where she lived before, right? Did you hear anything like that at the station?"

"No." He looks over at me and rolls his eyes. "Sergeant Johnson thinks it has to do with the home tour. I got the feeling he'd love to put you on the suspect list, but he knows better by now, I guess. The man is infuriating. I don't envy Ruiz working with him."

I sigh as I look out at the still water in the marsh along our way. "But Johnson was pretty right about the whole thing with the murder of Bell Jackson and the drugs being all about the good-ol'-boys network on Sophia. Even got himself promoted."

"You know what they say: 'Even a blind squirrel finds a nut every so often.'"

I snort. "As long as I'm not on the blind squirrel's list. Do they have any idea what the murderer was looking for at Jasmine's?"

"No. Speaking of a blind squirrel, could Jasmine have found out something about someone here and held it over their head? Made them mad enough to kill her?" He turns into the shopping center that houses our favorite Mexican restaurant. "I know you think I'm her biggest fan, but that was just about her organization of the tour and how invested she was in it being a success. I know she could be a royal pain. Maybe she stumbled onto someone doing something or being somewhere they shouldn't have been? Just an accident. She's the type that would be suspicious, dig into it."

We find a parking place and get out and start walking. The ringing of the Salvation Army bell at the Winn-Dixie down the way is a peaceful sound, and I wrap my arm around his whole arm, not just his hand. Craig smiles down at me, then pulls his arm out of mine and wraps it around my short wool coat. I tuck my head onto his shoulder as we walk. We don't talk, just listen to the sound of the bell on the chilly air.

At the door to the restaurant, I stop and pull away a bit. "Let's not talk about this during dinner. Let's talk about the kids coming and Christmas and, well, us."

He looks at me for a moment, really thinking, and then he slowly nods. "That's a good idea." We open the door and breathe in the spicy smells, hear the chatter, and the weight of the day seems to fall away.

It's just a regular ol' date night.

~~~~~~~

Our agreement lasted all through dinner. Through the drive home. Even through chatting with the officer seated in his car in front of our house. He was eating a hot sandwich his wife had just brought him, so we didn't talk long. He said everything had been quiet, and it stayed quiet as we walked in the back door. Craig plugged in the lights for the trees and lit a couple candles while I made us the hot chocolate we'd discussed after dinner. It was a spell neither of us wanted to break as we settled on the couch. I told Alexa to play smooth Christmas jazz and then leaned back to settle into Craig's arm. We'd talked about us, well, everything except...

"I think you should move upstairs."

He doesn't move or say anything, but he doesn't seem surprised. I'm glad I can't see his face. What if he—

"You know, this is good," he begins. "You and me. Without the kids. Without my job. I think we're going to be fine, but—" His phone rings, and we're surprised because the phones have been so silent all night.

We separate so he can reach his phone in his back pocket. "It's Detective Ruiz." He answers and puts the call on speaker. "Hi. I'm here with Jewel; she's listening. What's going on?"

"Good. I wanted to ask you both something. Have you ever heard of a woman named Pam Ferguson?"

Craig says, "No," and I echo him.

"No. Is she a suspect?"

"The name rings no bells? Would you mind calling your friends—you know the ones—and then calling me back?"

"Oh, okay," I say as I scoot away from Craig, then stand to get my phone from my purse.

As I send a group text and wait for an

answer, Craig asks Ruiz if there are any other developments. I don't listen to them as the texts are coming in quickly—and with a bunch of questions. Annie just calls me, so I duck into the kitchen to hear her.

"Pam Ferguson, huh? No. Never heard of her. Why? Is she the murderer?"

"I don't know. I'll find out and let you know."

Annie groans. "Law, I've been hard-pressed to not call or even text you all night. We decided to let you and lover boy be alone. How are things? He seemed right worried about you this afternoon. Y'all feel good together. I think you're going to have a good night, especially if this Ferguson woman is in jail. Really have something to celebrate."

Her words pelt me like frozen sleet. I swallow and push the phone away from my ear as I mumble, "I've got to go, Annie." I check the text replies as I walk back into the living room and look at Craig. Okay, not at Craig but at his phone. I don't know if he heard what Annie said; she wasn't on speaker, but she is a loud talker. All I can think about is how he ended my request for him to move upstairs with the word "but."

"Nobody knows Pam Ferguson," I tell him.

"Listen, Jewel, I..."

"Call him back. Now." I sit in the chair across from the couch, my elbows on my knees, staring at his phone. He sighs as he hits redial.

"Hey, it's me," he says. "No. No one knows this woman."

"I didn't think so," Detective Ruiz replies on speaker, "but I wanted to check."

I blurt loudly, "Is she the murderer? Is she in jail?"

"No, Pam Ferguson is Jasmine Coffey's real name." He clears his throat, then adds, "And she's been to Sophia Island before."

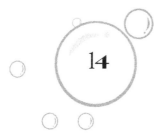

## 14

"Let me get this straight. I'm supposed to traipse around town with my boy toy? Just another cougar on the prowl around the holiday home tour. Me and my honey. That's your plan?"

Annie, Marisol, Lucy, and Tamela are standing on my porch, and they stare at me like they are nine years old again and I'm the new Barbie Dreamhouse in the department store window display. Or maybe they're just gawking at me, still in my robe at this hour. I give them the big ol' eye roll they deserve and pull the front door open further. "Y'all might as well come in."

"I've got fresh spanakopita from the farmers market," Lucy says sweetly. "I got there as they were setting up. I know it's your favorite."

Annie bustles ahead of everyone toward the kitchen. "I brought a fruit platter from Publix. Did y'all know they want you to order these ahead of time? Sure, I can march in there anytime and get a cake or cookies or pie, but try to walk in and get an arrangement of healthy fruit and they act like you have all the time in the world." She finally gets the hard plastic case opened. "I might've told a story about needing this for a grieving family to get them to bend the rules."

Tamela rolls her eyes. "You're good at getting people to bend the rules."

Annie beams. "I know."

Marisol shrugs off her wrap and puts a heavy bag on the table. "Here's juice, but the others convinced me champagne is not a good idea on such a busy day. I do hope you bought more than just those spinach pie things at the market," she says to Lucy. "I like something sweet to start the day."

Annie winks. "Something sweeter than Daniel?"

The two of them laugh, and I shake my head. I knew I shouldn't have begged off getting together last night after we found out Jasmine had another identity, but all I could think of was getting upstairs, closing my door, and getting the day behind me. Craig slept in his room. I slept in mine. Enough said about that.

Speaking of Craig… "Morning, ladies," he says as he walks into the room. He's also dressed for the day. I'm the only one not looking official and put together. He looks pointedly at me. "So, what do you think of their plan? You don't want to stay holed up here all day, do you? Upstairs by yourself?"

"They told you about me and Officer Cartle breezing around town all day? Like a couple of tourists?"

Tamela clarifies with a giggle. "Well, we didn't call him your boy toy when we talked to Craig."

Lucy sits at the table. "Most people will just figure he's one of your sons. Here, sit; I heated your spanakopita. Do you need more coffee?"

Marisol pours juice and gives me my options. "Daniel is assigning him to you whether you like it or not. None of us can go out with you today, so if you want to leave the house, it's with Officer Cartle in tow or"—her smile is sly and sexy—"with your friend Ty, who is just along for fun. We'll tell him not to dress too enticing.

Unless you prefer the uniform? Some women do."

"Stop it." I sashay to my place at the table. "Yes, I will take a refill of coffee. Here's my cup." I pull my robe tighter around me. "So, what's the rest of this plan you've all concocted?" I ask Lucy.

"Jasmine-slash-Pam and her husband owned a condo on the Island Resort property. One of the really nice ones."

"Her husband? She's married? She *was* married, I mean. Wow, I did miss a lot!"

Tamela shakes her head. "She was married, but no one knows where he is. He and Jasmine disappeared over a year ago."

"What?" I exclaim at all their resigned faces. Craig's knowing expression is particularly irritating. "Why do you already know all this?" I demand.

"I called Lucy this morning and asked what else they found out," he explains. "You hadn't made any noise upstairs, so I wasn't sure if you were even awake."

Everyone is suddenly busy with their breakfasts. I guess that answers everyone's question about how last night's sleeping arrangements went.

Marisol joins us at the table, deftly taking over the conversation. "I had no idea the Island Resort is so huge. Daniel had Aiden drive him down there last night, and he said it's over thirteen hundred acres. I went to a conference there years ago, but I had no idea about all the condos and houses. I just stayed in the hotel and conference center."

Craig props both elbows on the table. "So, are the police sure she had been to Sophia Island in the past, or did they just own this condo? Some people buy properties like that only as an investment. She really acted like she'd never been here, and she definitely never mentioned her husband. Was he at the condo at any time? Do they think he could've killed her?" He sits back in disgust. "This makes no sense. She's hiding out at a place where she owns property? And how rich was she? Those places are not cheap. Her condo here in town is one of the brand-new ones in the historic district; it's not cheap either."

Marisol shakes her head. "I don't think Daniel knows the answers to any of those questions. From what he's found out, they weren't on the run or wanted for anything. They just disappeared."

Lucy stands up. "Okay, we've got to get this show on the road. I need to get to the church to open up the manger display and you all have your places to get to. So, Jewel, your assignment, if you so choose to accept it, is to go to the other houses on the tour with Ty." She gives me a serious look. "Do not try to ditch Ty. He's a nice young man, and he's just doing his job."

Craig reaches out and grabs my hand. "Promise. Promise me you will stick with Ty."

"Okay, I promise." I jerk my hand back, acting like I'm starving for that last bite of my spinach-filled phyllo dough.

Annie adds some fruit to a bowl for herself. "Then y'all can go down to the resort property. I'm going to find out the address for Jasmine's condo, and I'll send it to you. You and Ty can snoop down there. I've got a Realtor friend who has some condos for sale there. She'll get me info so if anyone asks, you'll look like you have a reason to be there."

"And here's a picture of Jasmine, or Pam, for you to show around." Tamela takes a paper out of one of the files she's going through. (She takes the role of secretary for our group seriously.) "Show it to the housekeeping staff, at the front desk, and the restaurants."

"Yeah, like Ty's going to be fine with me doing that." I do take the picture, though. In it Jasmine's hair is longer and brown. No gray spikes which I thought gave her such a hard look. She has makeup on and I don't think I ever saw her wearing makeup. She obviously did try to look different. It makes me sad thinking of her living in hiding.

Craig also stands from the table, taking his dish to the sink and echoing my thoughts. "I don't think the picture is a good idea. That's more of a job for the police. How are you going to even get onto the property? Is this Realtor friend of yours going to meet her there, Annie?"

"Are you kidding? This is prime time for a Realtor. Lots of people get the itch to move here after walking through the Christmas homes." Annie shakes her head and bites a strawberry in half, then nods at Lucy. "That's her deal."

Lucy hands me a card over my shoulder. "Access is my department. Here you go. Tourist council ID. Gets you in anywhere. Act like you belong there; that's the first step to getting around a place like that." She pauses, her hand on my shoulder. "Mainly you're just looking around because the rest of us can't, but we're all going to have our ears and eyes open all over town. Then we'll get together tonight and talk. Meet back here at four thirty?"

As everyone agrees, they spread out, putting their coats back on and helping straighten up the kitchen for the Saturday tours. I get up and hurry to the stairs. Then, halfway up, I turn and ask loudly, "Do we know if we can take down the crime scene tape on the lawn and get rid of the flamingos?"

Craig yells from the downstairs bathroom, "No. It all stays in place, the police told me. I called again this morning."

I bend to look out the tall front windows. "Well, at least there's no fog this morning."

Tamela sighs. "Yeah, the fog made them look creepy. In the sunshine they just look downright mean."

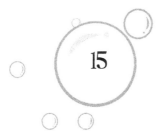

# 15

"So, what's up with the flamingos?" Ty asks as we get in my minivan, which Craig had parked out on the street so we didn't have to pull through the crowds.

Out the windshield, the pink birds face away from us, except for one that's fallen and now looks at us as if pleading for help from any passerby. "We think they're from our prankster," I say. "But who knows? Maybe the killer left them."

"Or the prankster *is* the killer."

"But that would mean the murderer has been hanging around for several weeks messing with us, so that's not it."

"Oh. I see," Ty says while pulling on his seat belt. "I completely understand what you're saying. You want it to be someone from out of town, just passing by or just here to do this one job; then they're long gone. I learned about that kind of thinking at the academy. Nobody wants a murderer to be a local, especially not a local they know."

I pull a U-turn in front of our house to go back toward the Ponce cottage. Besides theirs, the other houses are too far to walk to. We're almost to the cottage before I ask, "You think they could've been here all along?"

"All I'm saying is we don't know if they've just arrived or already lived here. Murder is a tricky thing. We can't settle on one idea right off the bat. We have to thoroughly examine every possibility. So this first house is where we found you yesterday, right? You didn't tour it then?"

"No, I just needed to talk to Craig. The Ponces are really nice, so I want to be sure and see their house. They've become close to Craig while he's helped them fix it up for the tour. I think he reminds them of the son they never had."

We park and get out. As we head up the stone walkway, I tell him, "You're right in between the ages my sons are, so I'm just going to treat you like one of them, okay?"

"I figured that was what was going on when the detective told me to wear street clothes. Do I look okay?" He's wearing a sport shirt and khakis, but he still looks like a police officer to me. Something about the way he stands.

"You look fine." I hurry down the path. This may sound weird, but I want to see the other homes, and while yesterday afternoon's captivity in my bedroom was great, that was enough solitude. In the spirit of the season I'm wearing a red, long-sleeve shirt with a white wool blazer, which I know I'll need to take off this afternoon. My pants are a dark plaid wool and only for wearing this time of year. They have a black background with white and green lines, then tiny, red lines that tie it in with my shirt. I've not had to buy any winter or fall clothes; living so long in the Midwest has filled my closets with those, although they do tend to be on the warm side. Like the lady I ran into yesterday said, I've got to get better at layering.

This early in the day there's no line, so we walk right into the house and tour it quickly. I wave at both Craig and Tamela, but I don't interrupt them as they are talking to others who are arriving for the tour. The biggest attraction is the collection of lighted, ceramic houses and shops spread throughout the downstairs. The town square is laid out on the dining room table. An ice skating scene graces a table behind the living room sofa. Along a window seat in the living room is a neighborhood scene, complete with kids on bikes, dogs, and a baby in an old-fashioned snowsuit. There's a fire station and a police station on a bookshelf in the narrow hallway, where Ty causes a bit of a bottleneck. He's fascinated by it.

Even so, fairly quickly we are walking to the car.

"That reminded me of my grandma's house," Ty says. "Everything felt really welcoming. Cozy. What did you think?"

"It was nice. A little crowded with stuff for my taste, but you're right. It felt like a grandma's house." I smile at him, and he smiles back. This might not be so bad. "The next house is not small at all, but it's really old too."

We drive out of our neighborhood, across Centre Street, and into the area surrounding the Catholic church that's been here since 1872. There's also a church school, and it's a very peaceful, beautiful area with many old homes. The one on the tour has been completely renovated, and it's the one I've been most excited to see. Lucy was a bit put out that Jasmine was able to get the owners to agree to participate this year. She said no one else had ever managed that. As I'm telling that to Officer Cartle, I wonder if there was a reason for that. Could the owners have known Jasmine from her previous visits to Sophia Island? Maybe they're friends from where they came from? Maybe she blackmailed them? Is this the murderers' home?

This keeping my mind open to all possibilities is exhausting.

Ty strides to the gate and opens it for me. I have to wonder if my sons are that polite. If they're not, I'm going to have to fix that while they're here. As I walk through, he whispers, "Let's see if we can find anything that connects the owners to the victim. Maybe they knew each other before and that's how she got them to be on the tour."

I come to a halt and stare at him. Did he just read my mind?

He stammers, "I mean, if that's okay with you? I'm kind of suspicious, always have been. I've always wanted to be a detective."

"Oh, Ty, that's very okay with me." I loop my arm through his. "Has anyone told you about our little mystery-solving group?"

He grins. "Like there are in books?"

As the docent holds open the front door at the top of the steps for us, I pat his arm. "Just like in the books."

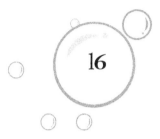

# 16

"Do you smell something?" I ask, but I can tell by the look on Ty's face that he does. We just got back to the van after the second home on the tour, but now we both jump back out.

We try to get a good look inside, but with the darkened windows and bright sunshine, it's hard to see anything in the van's interior.

"Here, give me your keys," he says. I meet him by the hood, and when I give them to him, he pushes a button on the fob and the rear door swings open. We cautiously walk around to look inside. "That's what I thought," he adds. "Run-of-the-mill stink bomb. Let's open the other doors."

As we're airing out the van, we look

all around, but no one is paying us any attention. Which tells you no one is anywhere near us or else they'd smell our situation. We'd parked on the same street as the new house on the tour but down the next block.

I lean on the front of my vehicle and text Craig to tell him our prankster is still active.

Ty leans on the hood beside me. "Detective Ruiz will be here soon. Thought I'd better call him and let him know." He shakes his head. "We left the van unlocked?"

"Apparently."

"Man, that's not going to look good. I'm supposed to be protecting you."

"I'm the one who had the keys. I just forgot, and they've never done anything to the cars. It's always been around the house." My phone beeps. "Craig's coming over too."

"It seems like a simple one, the kind kids use at school to get out of a test. The smell goes away pretty quickly, but at first they are horrible. They had to break it when they put it in; guess it's lucky we spent so much time in the house."

"Well, even though we didn't get to

meet the owners, we did find out that they have a condo on the resort where they're staying this weekend. Maybe they did know Jasmine. We can tell your boss that when he gets here."

He brightens up. "Yeah. We were focused on the case and just forgot to lock the car."

"Except I'm not so sure the police want us focusing on the case. I mean, at least not me."

"Oh yeah. That's probably true. There he is." Daniel bounds out of the car toward us.

My phone rings, so I take the opportunity to let the two officers chat. "Hey, Lucy."

"Your car was bombed?!"

"No," I'm quick to correct her. "A stink bomb, that's all!"

"Oh, good Lord. I've got to sit down." She breathes heavy for a moment. "We have a full house here at the church. People everywhere looking at all the mangers, and then a woman yelled, 'There's been a bombing downtown. My husband heard it on the police scanner!' Then Annie calls me—and you know how she talks so fast and says so much—but all I heard was your car and 'bomb,' and I put two and two together." She groans. "Oh, my stomach hurts. So you're fine?"

"I'm fine. Ty is fine. Detective Ruiz is here, and Craig just pulled up."

"Okay, this prankster has now jumped all over my last good nerve! But I've got to go, this place is a zoo! I've never seen it so crowded," she says as she hangs up.

I walk over to meet Craig, hug him, and then we join the officers.

Ruiz shakes Craig's hand, then reaches out both hands to cover mine as I stretch it out to greet him. "You're okay, right? Listen, I don't know what to think. Could this prankster be the murderer? Tell me your gut feelings."

"No," I say at the same time that Craig says, "Yes."

I turn to my husband. "Really? You think so?"

"Could be. I didn't say it is, but it would be a great way to get us confused. Or maybe the murderer is just using it as a distraction. Maybe this prank is from the killer to get us off track." He speaks to Ruiz, "Have you tracked down where the flamingos came from?"

Ruiz snorts. "Sort of. We did find out

they are not from an outfit that does the flamingo flocking. They are a mixed bag. Some are pretty old and beat-up. Some are brand-new. Looks to me like someone has been collecting them for a while." He shakes his head. "We've got the stink bomb bottle and will test it for fingerprints. We also have your details of the pranks, but if you think of anything else, no matter how small, let us know. I'm assuming neither of you saw anyone around the vehicle at any point?"

Ty, in his full police stance in his khakis and sport shirt, answers, "Not exactly. There were a lot of people in the vicinity. As you can see, it's all parallel parking along this street, but there have been cars pulling up and letting people out the entire time all along this stretch near the tour home, so lots of people near the car. Mrs. Mantelle parallel-parked and the car in front and behind us haven't moved, so I doubt their owners saw anyone."

"Let's get their plates and run them anyway. Get the plates of other cars in the area." Detective Ruiz looks down the street. "So that house with the line out front is the tour house, I assume?"

"Yes, so we didn't have the car in sight," Ty says.

"Locked?" his boss asks.

Ty swallows, then answers. "No, sir."

"But that's my fault," I say. "I had the keys."

"Officer Cartle knows whose fault it is." He glares at the young man. "Don't let it happen again."

"No, sir."

He growls, "Get those plate numbers."

Ty strides off.

Craig turns to me. "Why don't you come to the Ponces and finish off the day there?"

"No. This wasn't the murderer. I just know it. The murderer is long gone." I see the look crossing Detective Ruiz's face and flick my hand at him. "And I understand you think that's just because I don't want it to be a local person, and that is partly true, but I think this prankster is loving how seriously we are taking them. No, I'm going on about my day. With Ty hopefully, because none of this is his fault. He's doing a good job. Then I'll see everyone back at the house at four thirty." I whisper to the detective, "You're welcome to join us."

"I'll keep that in mind. Yes, I'll leave

Officer Cartle with you. Just be more aware, all right? I do not want to tell Charlie Greyson I—well, I don't want to tell him anything bad." He takes the paper filled with plate numbers from Ty. "Plans are unchanged, but no more missteps. None at all, understand?"

"Understood." Ty's still got my keys, and he says, "Why don't I drive?"

I nod as Craig holds out his hand. "Good idea, but take my truck. I'll take the van and air it out some more. Here's the keys."

"Yes, sir," Ty says, then adds, "Uh, we did find out the owners here have a condo at the resort. Maybe they knew the victim from before?"

I jump in. "Because this house has never ever been on the tour despite everyone trying. Then this year they tell Jasmine yes? That's fishy."

Craig provides more details. "The Kieffners. I met them. They're in their fifties, pretty wealthy. The house has been in the same family for years, but they just moved in a couple years ago. Parents moved to a condo in downtown Charleston. Didn't want the upkeep anymore. The current couple lived down at the resort before moving in here. Their parents weren't moving fast enough for them, and they were pretty vocal about it. Mad, actually. Felt they'd waited much too long to get to move in." He stares at the house, then says to Ruiz, "They seemed kind of high-strung. Might be worth a check. That is, if Jasmine actually spent time here on Sophia. Or did she just own the condo and never visit? I really find it hard to believe she was familiar with Sophia Island."

"Cartle, you can go wait in the truck." When the young man is gone, Ruiz looks at us. "She definitely spent time here, but I don't know if she ever left the resort. I get the feeling she went there to rest, not vacation. Her husband has also been here, but they didn't come at the same time from what we can figure out from the resort records."

I ask quietly, "Has there been any sign of her husband?"

"None. Before there weren't any official searches; her murder changed all of that. He's wanted as a person of interest. The only problem is no one has seen him for almost two years."

We think about that for a moment. Then Craig asks, "Do you think he's dead?"

Ruiz folds the paper Ty gave him and sticks it in his shirt pocket. "Let's hope not. He's our best hope at figuring some of this out."

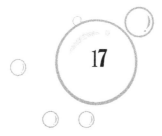

# 17

"You're alive!" Annie screeches as I walk in the glass doors of the modern, golf-course home where she's docent. It's our last stop on the tour and luckily on the Island Resort property, so meandering over to Jasmine's condo will be easy.

"Of course we're alive," I hiss at her as I brace for her hug. "Don't make such a scene."

After a tight squeeze, she holds me at arm's length and cocks an eyebrow. "This better be the end of all that pranking now that the police are involved!" she announces, just as loud as her initial pronouncement of my breathing.

Ty looks impressed. "Not a bad idea. Put the pranksters on notice. If it's truly just about being a pain in your sides, may-

161

be knowing the police are concerned will curtail their actions."

Annie hugs me again. This time when she speaks, she whispers. "Some real talkers are here. Best way to spread the word. Oh, and there's the living room set." She steers me toward the sunken living room in the middle of the bright house. I can't imagine living here, especially with the summer sun, as the room appears to be all glass. From the front see-through wall with the ten-foot-tall solid glass doors, you are looking out the back wall of glass, onto a golf course. It's beautiful, but the house looks dated, both inside and out; not at all like its neighboring houses, which exude understated Southern elegance. I can't remember when I last saw a sunken living room. Or this much glass.

"Living room set?" I whisper back.

"The one Jasmine insisted Shug borrow because hers was purple."

"Oh, that's right! I'd forgotten about all the furniture and fixture loans Jasmine set up."

The replacement furniture is cream-colored leather, a luxurious sectional with seating for a dozen. In this house, though, the same color of red velvet ribbon that in the older homes looks deep and old-fashioned looks almost black. Maybe it's the bright sunshine or the completely white-and-cream backdrop. The three Christmas trees I can see in the open floor plan are flocked with white spray in an attempt to make the trees look snow-covered. That was popular in the seventies, much like sunken living rooms. The carpet is white, the walls are white, and then all that glass. I'm beginning to think a purple living room set might help prevent snow blindness. I've now seen all the houses on the tour, and this one is awful.

I wonder out loud, "Jasmine approved all this?"

"Are you kidding?" a scratchy voice says behind me. "I didn't need no permission from her. Mainly I participated to stick it to our HOA. They forbade me from being on the tour. I showed them." I turn and see an angry woman, her hands on her hips and her chin jutted out. She looks like someone I would never mess with. Her face is draped in wrinkles, and unlike what Jimmy Buffett says, I do not think they are where the smiles have been. She earned these wrinkles with decades of scowling. Her nose curves downward as well. She sticks out a tanned hand with few wrinkles and tons of rings. "Shug Miller. You're that Mantelle woman." She laughs, and it just makes me more certain she is not to be messed with. "I know Pam loved jerking your chain."

Annie, Ty, and I all gasp. Ty encourages me to keep talking with a nod and even a prod in my back. I blurt, "So you knew Jasmine before?"

"I recognized her in town one day. Called her to come out and see about putting the house on the tour. Since our homeowners association forbids that kind of thing, she was out here lickety-split!" She laughs again. An audience gathers, which seems to feed our hostess's story. "Pam always believed in shaking things up, but she had no idea she was going to run into an old enemy."

"Um, maybe we should let the tour carry on and we can talk somewhere else?" I suggest as I feel the people around us closing in.

Ty steps between Shug and her audience and asks in a low voice, "Where did you know her from?" I think he's afraid to get her off her roll.

"Home. Rhode Island. Just outside

Providence. That place is lousy with home tours. So many historic houses and so many wannabes. Everyone wants to think they're the Newport Mansions." She rolls her eyes and her neck. "That poser Pam Ferguson was the queen of home tours there until everyone figured out what she was up to. I suspected she wasn't on the up and up, but still I tried to get our house there on the tour every year. Miss Snooty Pants didn't want our home. She called it gaudy. Not historic enough." Shug turns to step down into the sunken living room. "Then, lo and behold, the queen shows up here. Of all places! 'Course I didn't use my nickname when I called her, so she didn't know it was me she was coming to see."

Annie and Ty practically push me down the step behind her. I smack at their hands. "I'm going!" I hiss.

Shug sits in the middle of the new sectional couch and stares up at me. "She came running out here like her hair was on fire. She didn't even remember me." Her face purples, and she punches the pillow beside her. I can't help but notice it's the authentic color of red and would really look nice on my couch. Never mind.

I look away from the pillow and talk in

a low, calming voice. "But she put you on the tour here, so…"

Her smile is evil. Like when the Grinch—no, *exactly* like when the Grinch smiles. She kind of looks like him, from her body shape to her stuck-out bottom lip. I shiver because there is definitely evil in her voice when she growls, "Because I knew who she was. That she was using an alias. That got me on the tour." She spreads her arms. "And here I am. Also knew I could get some new furniture out of the deal." Her face looks genuinely happy for a moment. Then it all falls into wrinkles and scorn again. "Now she's dead, and I've lost all my leverage on this crappy island."

I've sat down gently on the couch, in the corner across from her, our knees only inches apart. Ty is seated on the arm behind me, and he's holding Annie back. She does not take kindly to people disparaging her island. Her silver eyebrows meet in the middle and her blue eyes have lost their sparkle. Her chin is capped by her deep frown and I consider us all lucky her mouth is folded shut into a frown.

I speak softly. "Leverage? Did you know something besides her name change?"

"That she was lying and she's a cheat."

She narrows her eyes. "Let them try and take this furniture back. They'll have to pry it from my cold, dead fingers."

Trying to hide my shudder doesn't work, but it does make her laugh and stick a stiff finger in my chest. "I can see how she dragged you around like a rag doll. You're a real pushover, ain't ya?" She raises her voice again and wiggles her eyebrows at me. "She sure did like your husband, though."

Annie has skirted around the room and now pops up on the other end of the huge sectional. Hands planted on her ample hips. "Shug, you knew she wasn't who she said she was? Why didn't you tell anyone?"

"Tell on her? Aren't you listening, old woman? I'd lose my leverage! Besides, she's kind of a hero."

"Hero?" Ty explodes. "Hero on what planet?"

Shug gives him a sly look. "Any planet where folks think pedophiles should be hung by their big toes till dead."

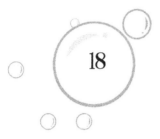

# 18

"Ty shut it down just like that," Annie says with a snap of her fingers. "Told us everything Shug was saying needed to be on the record. He called for a squad car and had her taken to the station."

Lucy rolls her eyes. "Oh, I bet Shug loved that! She's a drama queen if I've ever seen one. But she actually called Jasmine Pam? And what's that about a pedophile?"

I set a tray of store-bought sandwiches on the living room coffee table. "Help yourselves." I sit and face Lucy. "Yes, she did, and I don't know. I've been thinking, and I believe Shug was waiting for someone to tell it all to. We'd not been in the house five minutes when she was sidled up right beside us, spouting her info. She knew she had explosive stuff to say."

Marisol chooses her piece of sandwich and sits back on the couch. "Thanks for these, I'm starving. Well, from what I'm hearing, she is talking her head off at the station, but I don't know any of the details yet. Daniel did ask me to save him a couple pieces of sandwich, though, so I've got a feeling he may be stopping in here before long."

Tamela is seated on the edge of a chair with her laptop on her knees. "I can't find anything connecting Pam Ferguson with a pedophile, so whatever it was Shug was talking about, it wasn't in the news. I guess I never realized how big Providence, Rhode Island, is. They do have some beautiful old homes up there. And a lot of home tours."

"Craig?" I yell. He sticks his head out of the kitchen. "Didn't you think it was odd that the Millers' house was on the tour? It was awful. Didn't anyone question Jasmine about it?"

Annie exclaims, "Beyond awful! *I* sure wondered out loud why it was on the tour when we saw the houses on Thursday. Jasmine just shrugged and said, 'Tastes differ.' She even implied I was being a snob. Me! Everyone knows how humble I am!"

Tamela snickers but doesn't look up.

Probably a good idea. I hide my rolling eyes by calling out again. "Craig?" I repeat.

He's leaning in the kitchen doorway, a big grin facing our direction. "Just waiting on Miss Humble to finish. Yes, it was a different house from the others, but from what I can remember, Jasmine acted like it was a huge get. That the house was some kind of architectural marvel."

Marisol agrees, "That's right. It won awards or something."

"Like a million years ago," Lucy says as she scrolls on her phone. "Yeah, back in 1977 it was in an architectural magazine. And I do know her neighbors were not happy about it being on the tour, but she ignored them. She also threatened them with legal action."

"Oh, Shug is not above threatening lawsuits," Annie adds. "About any and everything. She moved here several years ago. Paid a royal fortune for that house and then set to making herself a real nuisance everywhere she went. Her husband seems like a nice guy, but I don't remember if I've ever spoken to him. He's one of those tech nerds that made a bundle on some invention."

Craig brings his sandwiches with him

into the living room. He's been busy adding jalapeños to his. He sets up a table tray in front of a side chair, then heads back to the kitchen. "I'm having a beer. Anyone else want one?"

Lucy raises her hand since her mouth is full. I raise mine, too, and then the front door opens and Eden strides in. "So this is where the party is!"

"I'm getting beers. Want one?" Craig asks her.

"Not yet. But hurry back. I've got news! Are these sandwiches for anyone? Aiden's hoping to come by in a bit, but he's already eaten at the station. He was starving, so they had pizza delivered, and I'm on my own for dinner."

"Absolutely," I say. "Here. There's room beside me."

The young woman squeezes in next to me on the couch and reaches for a sandwich and a napkin. "Downtown is a complete madhouse. The Jacksonville news crews reporting on the murder included shots of our charming town, and with this nice weather, it feels as crowded as the Shrimp Festival. I didn't say it to Aiden, but I don't think he's getting off at his normal time. That's probably why they got pizza." She jumps up. "I need a water. Can I get anything for anyone?"

Craig passes her at the kitchen door, but she's back quickly and settled in. After a long sip of water, which we all watch like she's performing a trick, she says, "Okay, here's what I found out helping Dad at the tattoo parlor this afternoon. Someone was buying up old flamingos on Facebook Marketplace a few months back. I went and researched it, and it was a woman from off the island. I messaged her, and she said she was doing it as a favor for a friend who doesn't have Facebook but was paid five dollars for each of them. She said Sergeant Johnson had already been out to talk to her this morning."

"But when we talked to Daniel this morning he didn't mention it," Craig says, frowning.

Lucy huffs. "I bet Johnson is keeping stuff from him. He likes to think he's Hercule Poirot when he's more like Barney Fife in Mayberry."

"I'm texting Daniel," his wife says.

Eden bites into a sandwich and groans with pleasure. "I've not eaten all day," she says with her mouth full but her hand hiding it.

It's quiet while the rest of us eat and drink. Then Lucy says, "Oh, Jewel, I need my tourist council ID back before I forget. I guess you didn't get to go out to the resort with Ty taking Shug in."

I get up and go to my small purse, which is in the kitchen. I take my beer with me for a little liquid courage as I walk back in and say, "Well, I know I promised but…"

"Jewel! You went out there alone, didn't you?" Craig accuses me.

Okay, he accuses me with reason. He knows me. "Yes, but I was really, really careful. I dropped Ty off, and it was too early to come home and too early to pick up the sandwiches, so I headed south and just drove around the resort."

Craig does not look happy. My suddenly quiet friends keep eating and drinking and let him handle things. "Just drove around? So you didn't get out of the car?"

"Well, of course I had to get out a bit. I needed to use the restroom, and the lobby of their building was open."

Tamela's forehead wrinkles. "They just let you come in off the street and use the bathroom there? I didn't realize that."

"I had the ID and followed Lucy's instructions. Acted like I belonged."

Lucy winks at me, then takes a serious tone. "Okay. I'd rather you'd not been alone, but there's nothing we can do about that now. So, did you learn anything?"

I sit back down and don't look at my husband. "An elevator was sitting there, open and waiting, so I went up for just a minute. Their condo has police tape across the door, but the cleaning lady I talked to had been in there earlier this week. She said it's been sitting there, completely unused, for a long time. All the staff have been talking, and just like Detective Ruiz said, Pam and her husband—his name is Joseph—were never there together. But when he was there, he had *company*."

"Ohh," Annie breathes. "You said 'company' like it means something. Like a girlfriend? Hookers? What?"

"No," I say with a frown. "She said it was like he was holding business meetings. That they ordered food for a dozen people and it wasn't party food. It was, well, like plain old sandwiches or pizza."

"What about when Jasmine was there?" Tamela chimes in.

"She had no idea. The meetings were

the only reason anyone remembered her husband being there. Apparently they left a mess and no extra tip ever. She said that's unusual. But…" I hold a finger up as I take a drink. "But I did run into one of their neighbors. She lives there, and she said she was shocked to find out Pam had been on the island at all. Even as a different person. She said when she knew her it was like she was hiding out. Pam brought her own food and only left to walk on the beach at sunrise. That's when this woman got to talk to her."

"Daniel is going—" Marisol tries to say, but I interrupt her to make it clear I did what I should have with the information.

"Yes, I've already sent him her name. I was very good about sharing everything I found out. And I wasn't killed." There's a knock, so I turn to the door, which slowly creaks open. Detective Ruiz quickly steps inside. "Speak of the devil," I greet him. "I was just telling everyone how I gave you all my information."

Daniel Ruiz looks at me, and then his eyes rush to his wife as he holds up his phone. "Just got a text from one of the guys that Sergeant Johnson is on his way over here. I don't think we should be here."

Lucy stands. "We can't let him think he has the upper hand and can't have you two scurrying around like scared rabbits." She picks up the plate of sandwiches. "Get rid of our beers and let's make this look more like an interview than a party."

Annie has moved to the window seat. "Better hurry. He just pulled up."

We're all back in place, the detective standing with the rest of us seated, looking up at him as he interrogates us. In the silence the song "Grandma Got Run Over by a Reindeer" starts playing, and our serious looks succumb to surprise. I don't think we realized the music was still playing under all our talking.

Tamela says solemnly, "This is Hert's favorite Christmas song." She adds with an exaggerated eye roll, "When that line comes on about should they open Grandma's gifts or send them back, he always yells with the kid singers, 'Take them back!'"

And that's how Sergeant Johnson stormed into our house to find us all belly-laughing, barely able to draw a breath.

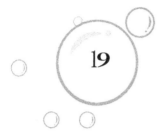

**19**

"It was interesting watching Johnson and Ruiz investigate in the same room last night," Lucy says as she drives away from the church parking lot on Sunday after service. We're headed to Annie's for lunch while the Christmas Home Tour committee has their wrap-up meeting. Craig made Lucy promise she'd be with me all afternoon, and after hearing more details of Jasmine's death, I'll make sure we keep that promise.

"Interesting in what way?" I turn in my seat. "I mean, I agree it was interesting, but I want to hear what you're thinking."

Lucy's mouth stretches into a big grin. "Oh my, isn't the marriage counseling giving you a whole new way of communicating? Anyway, Johnson is as blundering as ever, but he does have some good instincts as we discovered back in the fall. He's also figured out that we're not stupid, and I think that made him pay attention to the pranks at your house. I'm surprised he knew to even look on Facebook Marketplace, which is a plus in his column. Still, he's such a plodder. One foot slowly in front of his next foot, then drag the next foot forward. That Daniel, though—well, he's a firecracker. Seems to jump from one thought to the next and string things together quickly. Or, well, I hate to say it, but is he getting his cues from his wife?"

I jump on her question. "I noticed that too. And why is he only a detective? I looked it up last night. That's not very high up in rank, and he's not that young."

"Oh, yeah. That's true." Lucy thinks for a moment. "Maybe he did something else before joining the force. It's just weird to me how much he trusts us. And yet they didn't reach out to any of us when they first moved here even though Charlie told them all about us."

"Hey! That's right. She was on the committee with Craig, but that's it. And he knew Aiden, so he could've reached out to Annie through him at the very least."

Both our minds are churning, but we both settle down to not miss the view as we leave the more traveled roads and turn on the small, half-sand road to Annie's place.

Golden sunlight across the marsh deepens the blue of the water and the sky. It makes the brown marsh grasses glow. Everything feels so gentle this time of year here. Not like the harshness or sharpness of winter up north. This first Christmas on the coast is so different, and I'm wondering how the kids are going to feel about it, especially the boys, who will be staying here until the New Year.

Annie lives out on the marsh in a house she and her husband, Alan, built as a young couple over thirty years ago. They filled the house with the laughter and craziness of six children, but then when the oldest were in their teens, Alan passed away. The house is so beautiful, but with her youngest two moving out recently, I think Annie's feeling lonely. We all readily agreed to lunch here when she suggested it yesterday.

Her house sits way off the road behind a forest of small pine and palm trees. Her driveway is dirt and sand, and as we come out of the trees, our view opens up. Past the house lays the marsh, and the soft, blue sky reflects off the water. The whitewashed house with the tin roof looks like a picture in a Florida history book, like it's been here several generations, but then again, Annie says that's the way Alan planned it. It's a large, sprawling house with a porch wrapping all the way across the front. Tamela, Hert, and Ray are rocking on the porch, waiting on us.

Under her breath, Lucy says, "Ray looks awful comfortable in that rocker."

"You think he's staying here much?"

She gives me a highly arched eyebrow. "Well, it's not like you can ask something like that without sharing your own sleeping arrangements, is it?"

"Whatever," I answer and get out of her car. "Hey!" I shout. I do not wait for Lucy to catch up since she was being nosy. She's stepped back to her open trunk. I'm sure she's getting out something delicious, all in cute containers. It's not just her clothes that always match. Annie said not to bring anything for lunch, so I didn't. Lucy, meanwhile, said her mother wouldn't let her come empty-handed.

I've discovered having Southern manners can be quite burdensome at times.

Ray comes off the porch, and when we meet on the sidewalk, he gives me a quick hug. "Better go help Lucy before Annie gets on me!" he says as he hurries on.

See what I mean about the whole Southern manners thing? Ray is a large, sweet man who was born and raised in Sophia Beach. He lives off island on a family farm, where he runs Plantation Services, his large cleaning and sanitation business. His grown sons, and more than a hundred employees, work for him, and he's made no secret about the fact that he's ready to retire and settle down here with Annie. He's even said he'd happily leave the busyness and business of the farm behind him. All of their grown kids have known each other for years, and none of them have a problem with his plan.

Annie is apparently the only roadblock—a very formidable one, in fact—so Ray just bides his time. I guess how it shakes out all depends on just how lonely Annie ends up getting out here.

Hert gets up from his rocker and stretches his back as I walk up on the low porch. He steps to the door to open it for me. "So Craig won't be joining us, I hear. He's got to wrap up the tour committee?"

"Yep. Sounds like it'll be a long meeting. Does everyone feel as hungover as I do from all the work of the tour?"

Tamela laughs from her rocking chair. "I always do after one of the big festivals or events. And then I swear I'm not getting involved next time."

Hert rolls his eyes. "But we do! 'Cause that's what makes living in a little town like this fun. And then throw a murder in the middle of it? Well, it's like living in some novel!"

Tamela kicks her foot out at him. "Hert! That's rude." Then she adds, "But, well, anything else come out this morning? We found out Marisol and Daniel are Catholic. Saw them walking to Saint Michael's this morning on our way to church."

As Ray and Lucy join us, Hert says, "Also from the guys at the station I heard that Sergeant Johnson sure isn't a fan of the newest detective from North Carolina. Especially not after finding him at your house having a laugh fest last night."

Lucy huffs at him. "Well, that's your fault. That 'Grandma' song came on, and Tamela told us about your favorite line."

He shout-sings, "Send them back!", and we all laugh again.

"We better go see if Annie needs any help," I say as we all meander in the front door. "Are Cherry and Martin going to be able to come?"

Annie answers from the kitchen. "Sounds like it. She went in early to the hospital this morning and is getting off at noon."

Following her voice, and the delicious smells, I find my friend at the stove stirring a big pot.

"That smells delicious!" I enthuse. "But I don't recognize it."

"Brunswick stew. Ray makes the best. He came over and made it here yesterday so he didn't have to transport it. I've got cornbread and biscuits in the oven. Lucy insisted on bringing a dessert, so we've got two: my red velvet cake and whatever she and Birdie made." Annie lowers her voice. "She said Birdie wasn't up to coming. I don't think she's doing well at all."

"Me neither, but I hate to ask too much." Birdie is Lucy's mother, and in the months I've known her, she's slowed down considerably.

Annie puts an arm around my shoulders. "I'm so glad you moved here and let us all just invade your life. I didn't even know I needed some new blood in my life! Oh, I smell the biscuits!"

I step back to let her open the oven door as Lucy and Tamela enter the kitchen. "How can we help?"

"Put these in the basket with the poinsettia cloth. Cornbread needs another minute or two."

Lucy grabs a pot holder and takes the cookie sheet full of biscuits.

I move a large, red-and-green, crocheted pot holder for her to set the cookie sheet on. "Oh, those smell amazing. Craig is going to be so disappointed he missed this! I'm sure he's never had this soup either."

Annie gives me a mean look. "It's stew, not soup. And we'll send him home a Cool Whip bowl full. A *big* Cool Whip bowl, not the small one."

I smile. Annie's not as big on coordinated, cute food containers as some.

"Martin and Cherry are here!" Ray shouts from the front door. "And I finished getting the table set." Then softer we hear him say, "Ladies are that-a-way, Miss

Cherry. Martin come have a seat in a rocker until that dinner bell rings."

Cherry comes in the kitchen, and my heart jumps a bit at how much I've missed her this weekend.

"Cherry!" we all cry, and I'm reminded of the old television show *Cheers* and how they yelled the names of the regulars when they showed up in the tavern. It really feels great to be a part of a group like this. I'm still astonished at how we seemed to just jell. Lucy and Annie still have friends in so many different groups from their years of living on the island, Cherry has good friends from the hospital, and Hert's many interests have him and Tamela part of pretty much everything happening around Sophia. But this group feels special. Maybe it's the danger we've found ourselves in together. Or our shared interests in solving mysteries.

I have at times thought they were just humoring me, coddling the newcomer with the screwed-up marriage, but that's not really how it is. I know that now. I belong here. They know me and call me out. They laugh *with* me and *at* me.

Taking a deep breath, the spicy, tomatoey smell of the stew along with the warm sweetness of the biscuits and the earthiness of the cornbread is thick. I'm filled with the smells, my thoughts, and peace.

I think this is what home feels like.

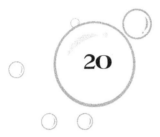

# 20

"It looks like a Cool Whip factory in there on Annie's countertop!" Ray says with a laugh. "She's pulled them bowls and lids outta the back of every cabinet in there, but we've got it all squared away for y'all to take home. I made two batches of stew yesterday, one here and one at the farm, so y'all have to take it home."

I know I have a big container to take home for Craig, but I'm not sure how he's going to like it. I've got to say, I won't be asking for the recipe, but I would like to be able to give Craig a bit of a heads-up. "So what exactly is in Brunswick stew?"

Ray shakes his big head of white hair and gives me a sly look. "Oh, what ain't in there! That's the real question. Roy Blount Jr. is a funny guy from Georgia. Wrote a bunch of books. He says, 'Brunswick stew is what happens when small mammals carrying ears of corn fall into barbeque pits.'" Everyone laughs—me not so freely. "But rest easy, mine's just got chicken and pork. Then there's the corn and lima beans. But it's the barbeque sauce you don't get in most stews. It's kind of my specialty, and it's from up near Brunswick. Hence the name."

Hert holds up his hand. "Well, now, you know Brunswick, Virginia, claims the stew too."

Ray jerks his head back and stares Hert down. "Well, they're wrong. Brunswick, Georgia, is where it comes from, and there's a big ol' pot for a statue that proves it."

Annie rolls her eyes. "He ain't lying. They got a statue of a pot. We took a day trip just to see it."

We're on the screened-in back porch, enjoying the warmth from a small heater. The women are wrapped in an assortment of blankets and afghans, and honestly, a nap seems like a great idea, but we've got detecting to do.

Ray walks over to Annie and puts his hand on the back of her neck. "Sugar, I'm going back to the farm while y'all have your talk. Kitchen is all cleaned up." He looks around the porch. "Good to see y'all today. Martin, you said you want a ride home?"

Cherry's husband stands quickly. "Yeah. I've got a work project I want to get started on. That sure was a fantastic meal, though I'm already regretting my double portion of banana pudding." He pats his stomach and laughs as he follows Ray off the porch and we all say goodbye.

"Wait, I have a question," I call after them. "Not about the actual crime stuff, but Ray, you're from here. Do we have flamingos here? Real flamingos."

Ray stops at the door going inside and takes a step back toward us. "Naw, not really. Every so often a hurricane will blow some off track, and someone will see them. I've heard of them as far north as the Carolinas. Now with everyone carrying around phones you see some pictures, but I'm even skeptical of those."

Lucy agrees. "What we get a lot of people taking pictures of are roseate spoonbills, which do come this far north in the warmer months. They're pink but look more like pelicans than flamingos in my opinion. But the tourist council gets asked about them a lot, people claiming they saw flamingos."

"Look out there," Annie says, standing and pointing out the screen. "See that big dead tree at the edge of the water? One summer I had a flock of pink spoonbills there for weeks. From away they're so pretty, but up close not so much. They look bald and gawky."

Everyone chimes in about their spotting of the pink birds or their not spotting of them.

"Well, I'm going to be looking this summer. Thanks, Ray," I say with a wave. "Now, back to the pink birds of the hour."

Martin and Ray nod, wave, and shuffle on into the house, pulling the door closed behind them.

Annie and Cherry share a look, and Annie asks, "Martin still having trouble with the mess from this past fall? With Jo and the drugs?"

Cherry nods. "He has trouble believing she was mixed up in all that. He's grateful that our group was instrumental in it all unraveling, and he's happy we were involved because it got Jo out safely, but he doesn't like knowing how dangerous it all was. He said for now he'd just as soon not know."

"Ray simply feels ashamed," Annie says with a frown, "to be mixed up with that mess. And knowing it put one of his good, lifelong friends in prison is just too much. It all took a toll on him. Plus, being kicked off the city council because of it all really sticks in his craw, so he's just keeping his head down and said he'd hear what all we talk about later."

Lucy pats her friend's leg. "He's a good man." She shoots me a questioning look, but I'm not asking anything more about Annie's relationship.

I clear my throat. "Okay, before I fall asleep from all that wonderful food, I've got to talk about what we found out last night. Jasmine was stabbed four times, Johnson told us, and left to bleed out, but they have no idea where? How can that much blood go unnoticed?"

Hert motions at his wife. "Tamela has the notes I took talking to buddies at the station. I'd rather we look at that before Mrs. Ruiz shows up. The guys don't want her to know they tell me stuff. They're afraid it'll get back to her husband."

Tamela slaps the papers against her leg.

"She's not Mrs. Ruiz. She's Mrs.—wait, does she call herself Mrs.? Is she Mrs. Sanchez or Ms. Sanchez?"

Cherry claps her hands. "I'm too tired for that. Marisol. Her name is Marisol. Give him the notes."

Hert reads, "Four stab wounds earlier in the evening. There would've been a lot of blood, but there's none in her apartment or where she was found. They don't have the weapon either, but they don't think there's anything special about it. Except it was used to kill a person." He studies the paper, not wanting to look at us. "It probably took a while for her to die."

Annie looks sick to her stomach. "Maybe Ray's right. This is just so gruesome."

We take a pause, and I look out at the water, studying the ripples, the solitary birds, the slow-moving clouds. "But I need to know that what happened is not just ignored or left unsolved. Marisol actually told me last night that Daniel was glad to have people like us so concerned. In a lot communities no one wants to really know what happens. No one cares. I've been listening to some true crime podcasts, and I've got to say I'm shocked how many things never get solved."

"Really? I mean, I believe you about unsolved crimes," Lucy says, "but Marisol really said that? The detective is glad we're interested?"

"Yes. So I think we should keep asking questions. If nothing else just to let the police know we're not going to look the other way or forget."

Cherry sighs. "I agree. I can't help but think of Jo being mixed up with that idiot boy who just happened to get involved with major drug dealers. She could've ended up in jail or dead."

Annie sits up straighter and shakes herself. "Y'all are right. I'm just tired and haven't had time to think through everything. It's all happened so fast. First thing I want to know is what was all that about a pedophile? Do we know what Shug told the police?"

Hert shakes his head. "I don't have that. Tamela said Ruiz and Johnson wouldn't talk about it last night. Tamela can't find anything on the internet, and we all know if it was there she would've found it."

Tamela blushes as she looks up at her husband. He's sitting on a stool near her, and he gives her a wink.

"I think we can just ask Shug," Annie proposes. "I'll offer to bring her some cake. I bet she tells us everything."

Cherry raises her hand. "I'm going to have to go home soon. I can't stay awake much longer—it's been a long weekend at the hospital—but if y'all want to go over there, be my guests. You can fill me in later. I do want to know if there's anything more about the prankster. The stink bomb or the flamingos or anything?"

"No," I say. "Although Daniel said to Craig last night when he was leaving that he thought they'd have a breakthrough soon."

We all just look at each other, and then Annie dials a number on her phone. "Shug, me and the girls are headed over there with some homemade red velvet cake for you and Donald. You'll be there for a bit?"

She listens, then hangs up and stands. "Says she's putting on a pot of coffee and looking forward to a chat."

Cherry stands and stretches. "Well, if she's going to have coffee I think I'll be okay. I can always sleep later. Besides, I need to see this house."

"Well, I didn't know it was you!" Hert says when the Millers' front door opens. "Ace, I don't think I even knew your last name." He pushes Tamela ahead of him. "Honey, this is Ace from the model rail-road club."

The man holding the door open stares at Hert. "Oh, uh, Stout, right? You're with this group. Mystery solvers, I guess?"

"Something like that. Hert," he says, shaking hands. "This is my wife, Tamela."

The rest of us introduce ourselves as we walk into the large entranceway. The decorating is all the same as yesterday. Everyone except Cherry has already seen it, so we cover for her to stare to her heart's content.

"Shug is in the kitchen," Donald says. "Guess that's the cake she said you were bringing?"

"Sure is!" Annie says as she sails on ahead. "Shug, where do you want us?"

We don't take long to get seated as the only one eating cake is Shug. Donald, or Ace, is a very tall, broad-shouldered man with only a little gray-blonde hair left. He's wearing a heavy, Nordic-looking sweater and dress slacks. He explains he doesn't eat sweets as he loads his coffee with sugar and then says he's going downstairs while we talk. "Want to come along, Stout? You can see my new train layout."

Hert takes a moment to decide, but it doesn't take long, and then it's just us five ladies and Shug around their large dining room table.

"This is good," Shug says. "I'm not a huge fan of eating food color, and I've found some red velvet cakes tend to just taste like food coloring, but this is good." Now, along with looking like the Grinch, her teeth are red when she grins at us. "So it's been an exciting weekend, hasn't it?"

"Tiring too." I chuckle, looking away toward her living room. "But it's nice to have the house decorated this far ahead of the holiday. Our kids are all coming in next week."

Shug pauses. "They're coming here for Christmas? Why, it's like summer. Who'd stay here for the holidays? We're headed home as soon as we get the car packed. I'd never make my kids come *here* for Christmas." She's hunched over her cake, and now she's added her grinchy attitude toward my family get-together.

"Well, I like not freezing and not having to shovel sidewalks!" I spout, then suffer a kick to my shin from Lucy, who leans between me and our host.

"Oh, you are so right, Shug, but those of us who have always lived down here don't know any better. How many kids do you have?"

"Two. Both still in the Northeast. Brendie is a professor at a university in Massachusetts, and Don Jr. is still in Providence. He and his wife have a home in East Greenwich. You can bet little Pammy Ferguson would jump at the chance to have his home on some stupid tour." Her brow wrinkles, and she stops herself. "I mean, if she wasn't dead. Anyway, Donny's done very well. Everyone knows you can't do better than New England for education. It's for sure my Brendie wouldn't dare be caught teaching down here."

I don't have a dog in this fight, as Annie would say, but I can see hackles rising, so I jump back into the fray. "So Pam Ferguson was someone you knew pretty well back in Rhode Island?"

Shug pushes her dessert plate away from her, then leans both elbows on the massive, dark-wood dining room table. "Of course. I already told you that. We ran in the same circles; she just didn't want to acknowledge it. She wanted to be one of the movers and shakers, but those circles are always hard to break into. Especially in that area. I thought it would be easier down here, but there's just as many snooty people here as anywhere." She gives Lucy the stink eye, but I lay a restraining hand on Lucy's leg. Much nicer than a kick to the shin, I think.

Annie cuts to the chase. "You said she's your hero. Something about a pedophile?"

Shug looks around. "I probably shouldn't have said that around so many people yesterday. I'm kinda hoping Ace doesn't hear that I said anything. He says those people can be ruthless."

Annie leans closer. "Pedophiles?"

Lifting one shoulder in a partial shrug, Shug looks around again before nodding. "And the *people* around them." She stretches her eyes wide, like we should know what she means, but I don't think we do.

Annie whispers, "Other pedophiles?"

Shug whispers back, "The Mafia."

We all sit back in our chairs. Tamela squints at her. "Like the New York Mafia? Like in *The Godfather*? Or *Sopranos*?"

"You bunch of hillbillies! You don't know. You're looking at me like that buffoon Johnson at the police station. I probably shouldn't say anything more," she mumbles as she bows her head. Then she slowly lifts it and looks at each of us. "Unless you believe me…" She continues looking at each one of us one at a time, as if she's trying to read our levels of sincerity.

Cherry is sitting across from Lucy, Annie, and me and next to Shug. She reaches out her hand and lays it on Shug's forearm. "We are here because we believe you have something that needs to be said. You're right that we don't know much about that world, but we'll listen. We will definitely listen." Then, breaking her eye contact with our hostess, she stares at Annie, the one of us who has the hardest time just listening. I feel rather than see Annie's indignation, but the rest of us solemnly nod.

For just a moment, there's a glimmer in Shug's eyes that I don't like, much like when the Grinch sends little Cindy Lou Who back to bed with her glass of water.

"Okay," she says. "Pam was a hard worker, but she just could not get accepted by the hoity-toity women she chased after. That is, until she got that furniture store involved with some of the home tours. Like with my couch in there. All of a sudden they wanted her help on all the tours. Well, not the big, established ones, but in places like our area of the city, which was trying to get things cleaned up a bit. Raise our home values. I wouldn't exactly call it kickbacks with her arrangements, but there was some kind of con going on. Whether it was just free advertising or maybe the merchandise was stolen or there was some kind of quid pro quo, I don't know."

When she pauses to take a sip of coffee, I ask, "Is it the same company she was working with here?"

She nods. "Probably. Just a name change. I told the police all this, so I have a feeling they are all over that little meeting your husband is holding over there at your place this afternoon."

Surprised, I blurt, "How did you know it was at our house?" Craig offered to hold the final Christmas Home Tour meeting at our place since they couldn't meet at Jasmine's condo and they didn't want to meet in a public place, but I didn't think other people knew.

There's that smirk. "Oh, this place is a breeze to plumb for secrets after living in New England my whole life. People here will tell you everything they've ever known if you just give them the chance. Never seen people so ready to spill their guts." She stops and thinks. "Hmm, maybe that's why the Mafia never worked out so well down here."

Cherry gets her attention again. "So you told all this to the police, and I'm sure they're checking into all the possibilities for fraud and whatnot. But I'm a nurse, and I take care of a lot of children. I want to hear about the other allegations."

"That is the crux of the matter, isn't it?" Shug draws in a breath, then lets it out. "Now I'm not saying Pam's husband, Joe, was a pedophile himself. Matter of fact, I'd doubt it because he was real successful in his business. But then you never know, right? Anyway, the only reason I know this is because she showed up at a meeting of the historical preservation society we were both in, and she was upset. Like I said, I was trying to get our house there on her latest tour, so I was paying close attention to her. When she got up and ran to the bathroom, I followed her. To offer help."

Annie harrumphs beside me, but I cover it with a quick cough. I'm sure none of us believe helping was Shug's main goal.

"There she was, crying. Not even in a stall. First she was blubbering about the disgusting stuff she saw on the computer. Then all of a sudden she yelled at me to leave her alone. So I did." She turns her attention to the crumbs on her empty plate.

Cherry's tap on Shug's arm isn't as gentle this time. "And? What then?"

"Well, that was the last time she was around. I finally put two and two together when I heard her husband had skipped town too. You've got to understand there are just some things people don't look into too closely, you know? Even the officials. And the disappearance of the Fergusons was one of those things."

Lucy blurts, "But what about a pedophile in all this?"

"Oh, that was pretty well known not too long after he ran off. Nobody went to jail for it, you understand, but Joseph Ferguson was the money man behind a large-scale pornographic ring is what everyone was saying. A lot of it was pictures of kids from what I heard. Then, when they both disappeared, I figured they'd been killed and dumped in the river."

We're all quiet, processing this awful

turn of events. Then Annie asks, "But you said something about her being a hero?"

"Oh! That's right. I'd forgotten I told you guys that. And now that I think about it, she probably wasn't telling the truth."

"Jasmine? I mean, Pam?" Tamela asks. I noticed she quit taking notes a while ago. I'm not surprised. This has been almost impossible to follow.

"Well, I guess she was Jasmine at that point. See, when I got her over here and then reminded her I knew her, she told me she didn't leave with Joseph. Matter of fact, she was hiding out from him."

"Did she say why?"

Shug tilts her head at Lucy's question. "Why she disappeared or why she was hiding from her husband?"

Lucy is exasperated. "Either. Both. I don't care."

Shug grumbles. "Yep. You've always looked high-strung." She sighs. "Guess it was the same answer for both. She downloaded a bunch of stuff from their computer by accident onto a thumb drive. That's when she found out what he was doing. She said she just drove and drove for a while. A couple months. She stayed in some other places, but she never contacted him, and she said he never contacted her. She figured once the people at the top realized he'd lost a bunch of his scuzzy material, they killed him and dumped him in the river."

We are now all on the same page with Shug, and it's like a jolt of lightning has gone through the room.

Cherry says in her most nurse-like, 'don't mess around with me' voice, "So she had the thumb drive with her all this time."

Shug shrugs. "The police said they didn't find it."

Tamela rolls her eyes. "No duh. The killer took it!"

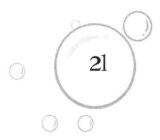

## 21

"Looks like you were right," Daniel Ruiz says when Lucy and I enter my living room. We'd come in the back door and gone straight to the kitchen with the containers of food and her huge bowl of banana pudding, which was half gone. We left Craig sampling it while we walked into the living room to find Detective Ruiz looking relieved. "It appears the murderer *was* from out of state, so now all you have to fear is your annoying prankster."

Craig had called on our way home to tell me we had visitors and that the police had solved the murder.

Marisol rushes to me and wraps me in a hug, then pulls back to look at me. "No murderer to find here! But we will not rest until whoever is pulling these pranks is found."

"I hope you're right." I turn to fall into my favorite lounger chair. "So, was it her husband they think killed her?"

Daniel shakes his head. "They won't give us any details, just that they've got it handled. I'm not surprised; Providence has a lot of connections to parties that are best not messed with by outsiders. But they assured us it's all taken care of and we have nothing to worry about. Sounds like Ferguson was involved with these unsavory parties through his financial management business."

I sigh. "That's basically what Shug said too. Lots of stuff about the Mafia. I wonder why she trusted the furniture company to not tell them where she was? I think she was tired of hiding. So I guess the bad guys found the thumb drive, killed Jasmine, and dumped her here at our house just for fun?"

Marisol and Daniel look at me, confused.

Lucy shrugs as she takes a seat on the couch. "Yeah, this is what Miss Jewel obsessed over the whole way home. Says the whole thing doesn't feel right, but I think it's because we're all exhausted from the tour. Plus, being with Shug Miller all afternoon does a job on your brain."

"There's banana pudding in here. Anyone interested?" Craig yells.

Lucy and I both groan a no in that direction, but Marisol and Daniel don't hesitate to check it out. As they hurry to the kitchen, I think they're disappointed at my reaction to their happy news of there being no murderer to worry about.

"I should not have sat down," Lucy says.

"I told you I could carry it all in." Then I whisper, "But I'm glad you're here. I want to get a read on them. Oh, but Birdie will be expecting you."

"Two friends have been there all afternoon with her. I invited them over for the extra banana pudding we made. They've texted me all along, and they have been having a great time." She talks louder as we're joined by the three with their bowls of thick, homemade pudding, vanilla wafers, and sliced bananas all covered with stiff meringue lightly browned in Lucy's oven.

She smiles at them. "The meringue

may be a little tough since it's several hours old now and has been carted all over."

The only answer is appreciative nods and fast-moving spoons. Craig finally comes up for air. "I'm starving. Who knew our meeting could go on so long? What a disaster."

Marisol's laugh is dark. "I think Mrs. Partridge from the museum would've killed Jasmine if she wasn't already dead. Mrs. Partridge talked to some of her counterparts in the Providence, Rhode Island, area and spent quite a few hours commiserating with them. Pam Ferguson was a nightmare up there, too, apparently. Pam, or Jasmine, caught us at just the right moment. Too short on time to do our due diligence. But we have all learned our lesson."

"Oh, and all our outdoor furniture we were keeping for a few months?" Craig points his spoon at me. "No longer part of the plan. The furniture store owner is throwing Jasmine under every bus he can find. Swears he was promised full payment for everything. He's sending a truck tomorrow, and it's all going back."

"Glad I'm not the one who has to tell Shug Miller she's losing her fancy couch,"

Lucy says. "So no reason to suspect the furniture people?"

Daniel frowns. "With the murder? No. The Providence police are positive it all had to do with Joseph Ferguson's illegal activity. They said this closes several open cases. They dismissed Mrs. Miller's accusations about the pedophilic material on the thumb drive. They said it was just financial dealings with Ferguson's company. But it would've meant jail time for him, so that's why he, or some of his associates, killed her when they found her. How exactly they think she was found, they won't say. People do get sloppy when they've been in hiding for a while, and it sounds like Jasmine did just that. Plus, if her husband did have dealings with the Mafia, they don't stop looking."

"Do the police have any leads on where he could be? If he's actually alive?" I ask.

"They said they should have the killer in custody in a matter of days; whether it's Ferguson or not, I don't know. But they were full of high praise for our department, so Sergeant Johnson is in an especially good mood."

Marisol scoots to the edge of her chair and pats her husband's knee. "Quite a feather in your cap too. I'm so proud of you. Solved your first murder case in a weekend."

He bites his lower lip and looks down, then quickly looks back up. "The speed of the resolution was totally due to our community partners, and I'm talking about you folks. Shug Miller would've hopefully eventually reported what she knew, but who knows how long it would've taken her. And Marisol is right; we are going to figure out this prankster thing. I promise." He stands up. "But right now it's time to go home." As we stand, he concentrates on me. "I agree; it is weird the body was dumped here. But maybe the flamingos caught the murderer's attention, or maybe Jasmine mentioned your house being on the tour at some point. One of the hardest things in police work is figuring out when something is just a coincidence and not a clue."

None of us are moving very fast, so it takes a while for our guests to be gone and for it to be just Craig and me sitting alone in the living room.

He chuckles. "I've been in some hellacious meetings with angry contractors and big, scary construction guys, but they were cakewalks compared to that mess this afternoon. And what was I thinking having it here? I couldn't even walk out!"

My head is laid back, and my feet are up. There's a soft blanket across my lap, and everything is safe and warm, but I can't get comfortable.

"Something's just not right," I finally grumble out loud.

Craig doesn't answer me. After a moment I open my eyes, raise my head, and look for him, sure that he's left the room. But no, there he is, in the same reclining position as I am, but on the couch. He's staring straight at me.

"What?" I ask. "What are you thinking?"

"Don't move and be quiet," he whispers. "There's someone on the porch."

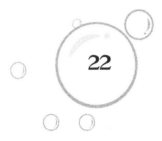

# 22

"Call 911," Craig says quietly as he points to my phone, which is lying on the table beside me. "Move slowly. Act like we don't know they're there, and maybe they won't go away." He puts his feet down, slides to the edge of the couch, and says louder, "I'm making a decaf coffee. You want one?"

I shake my head, trying to concentrate on dialing. With surging adrenaline, fear, and yet half asleep, my fingers fumble to dial the three numbers. "This is Jewel Mantelle," I murmur, "and there's someone sneaking around on our porch. Yes, where the flamingos are." The operator wants to keep talking, but I hang up because I see Craig grab a large umbrella from the kitchen closet. "What are you doing?" I hiss.

He motions for me to sit still as he creeps to the front door.

"I'm not sitting here—"

Then a quiet knock on the door makes me yelp and Craig jump back. We don't breathe, and the knocking comes again. As he steps toward the door, this time I'm up out of the chair and on his heels.

"Who is it?" he half shouts and half growls.

"Galena Bellington."

We look at each other.

Craig whispers, "Frank's wife?"

Craig spent summers here with his great-aunt and one friend he made who is still here—Frank Bellington. I don't think they've talked to each other since Craig retired and now lives here full-time, though. Frank and his wife are snooty, pretentious, and better than us.

Just ask them. They'll tell you.

I put my hand on his shoulder and say, "Maybe something is wrong with Frank? Bellington Manor is just around the corner. Let her in."

He opens the door. She shoves past

him, his umbrella, and me. He shuts the door, and we turn.

There in the midst of all our holiday finery—the lit trees, fragrant candles, and cozy setting—is a woman who always looks in control and superior. Except she doesn't now.

"No one can know I'm here," she demands, though her usual queenly tone is missing. It's more like she's pleading with us. "Please don't tell anyone. Don't call the police. Oh, please don't call the police. I need to tell you something about the pranks."

I hold up my phone and shrug in apology at the same time there's a siren outside. Galena is a beautiful woman. Her short, brown hair is cut in a perfect style to swoop over her eyes. Her clothes are always perfectly fit and styled. Even now, with tears ruining her makeup and sneakers instead of heels, she looks like a classic damsel in distress as horror overtakes her. She's wearing a pink plaid wool skirt and a tailored white blouse, but on top of that she has a big, black jacket. I bet it is her husband's. It's too big and plain for her. She actually looks a little pathetic, and I push my own husband toward the door. "Tell them it's okay."

"I'll handle it," Craig says as he steps out onto the porch, pulling the door shut behind him.

"You want to sit down?" I motion toward the couch as I move to the end and sit in a high-backed wing chair. She ignores the couch and takes the other wing chair, which I'd imagined Craig taking. Upset, in the middle of the night, wearing a man's raincoat, she's still Galena Bellington and will take the best seat in the house as she so richly deserves. Again, just ask her.

We wait in silence, but the longer I sit here, the less sympathy I feel. I don't want to talk to her, and I definitely don't want to talk to her without a witness, which is why I'm waiting for Craig. I do, however, have time to wonder why exactly I distrust her so much. Her mother-in-law, Charlotte Bellington, is in our lunch group. She can't stand her daughter-in-law, but then again, few people can stand Charlotte. She's mean and devious, but she is kind of a friend. Her opinion of Galena probably began my distrust of her. I've been to a couple cocktail parties at Bellington Manor, the huge house where Frank and

Galena live and run a very successful historic inn. Those parties are all about being seen with the important, beautiful people of Sophia Island. They are not fun. The parties or the people.

At those parties I've met a couple of pretty shady people who did some pretty nasty stuff. Galena might not have caused the nastiness, but she wined and dined the people that did. She's like the second-in-command of the mean girls. Yep, that's it. She's a mean girl. I'm surprised I hadn't thought of her in connection with the pranks before now.

Our heads turn as Craig steps back inside. "Okay, luckily it was Aiden, and he trusted you weren't being held hostage and that it was a false alarm. I told him it was a neighborhood cat." He chuckles and then comes to sit on the couch, right in the center of us. "So. Galena. You know something about the pranks?"

And then I have it. To be the second-in-command there has to be a leader. An instigator. And I remember who Galena's best friend is. "You and Fiona Greyson are behind all the pranks, aren't you?"

She draws in a deep breath, then releases it. "Yes. You got Charlie put in prison.

Do you have any idea how that made Fiona look? How it made her feel?"

Craig is struggling to catch up. I don't believe he ever met Fiona, Charlie Greyson's wife. She strung Charlie along like a battered puppy dog. Everyone talked about it: Charlie, a police officer, whipped into submission by his high school girlfriend–turned–wife.

"How it made *her* feel?" I whine. "Oh, poor, poor Fiona. Maybe she should save a tear or two for Charlie. He's the one in prison." My anger boils over. "Because he confessed!"

Craig holds a hand out to me. "Wait, I'm trying to figure this out, okay? Give me a minute." He turns toward Galena. "You did all that because you thought Jewel was responsible for Charlie Greyson going to jail?"

She sinks into the chair. "Well, Fiona—"

"Says jump and you ask how high. You are all disgusting." I cross my arms, then cross my legs and shut myself off from this conversation. I can't stand having her here in my house. I don't have to talk to her on top of it.

Craig waits a beat, then asks, "So,

where's Fiona? Why isn't she here confessing with you?"

"Because I'm not really confessing. I need you to tell the police something for me."

"Oh, you need *us* to do something for *you*!" And I'm back in the conversation.

"Fiona can't know I came here. But, well, the flamingos?" She squints, and all the wrinkles she so expertly hides show themselves. "I did those. I didn't do everything, and I'm not telling you the names of our other friends. No need for this to get out of hand."

Crossed arms and legs; I'm out again. I just can't deal with her!

Craig laughs. "Oh, it's already well out of hand. This is—well, go ahead what were you saying." He gives me a look that says we need to hear her out before we lower the boom on her.

I breathe in and out of my nose and wait as she seems to go back to the night of the flamingos in her mind. Her face moves through several emotions, all working hard against her expensive cosmetics and Botox injections.

"So… I was here that night, but the Santa hats kept blowing off the flamingos, so I left and came back with some glue. It apparently worked pretty well since I see most of the hats are still on, but I walked over since the glue was all I was carrying. Earlier I'd had to drive with the flamingos in the back of the SUV." She can't hold back a prideful grin. "I can't believe how many we managed—"

Craig stops her by sticking his hand up in her direction. "We don't care. Just say what you came to say."

She licks her lips and smooths her swooped bangs back. "Right. So I had just glued the hats on, and then I kneeled over by the big tree to wipe my hands on the wet grass. I'd gotten some glue on them. Anyway, that's when the car pulled up. I stayed hunched down because I just knew it was the police. I couldn't see what they were doing, but I heard them grunting like they were working. Then when their car door closed and they started off, I stepped out to walk home, but…"

"But what? Say it," Craig urges.

"There was a woman lying there. I swear I just thought she was drunk, and maybe someone else was pranking you. It was kind of funny, her hugging a flamingo to her chest like that, you know."

"Funny? You thought a murdered woman was funny?" I'm sputtering, so I just close my mouth and try to release tension from my shoulders.

Craig scoots down the couch closer to us. "Galena, have you told anyone else about this? You realize you are so lucky you weren't hurt. What if they'd seen you?" He gets choked up and sits back on the couch.

Her eyes are shiny, and her mouth is trembling. "I know. I've tried to forget it. I took some of my headache pills and went to bed all day Friday and yesterday. Everyone was busy with the tour stuff, so I could just lie low. Then last night I remembered something kind of important. I couldn't think of who to tell, but you do that mystery stuff, right?"

She's staring at me, and I'm speechless. I nod, then unfold my arms as all my strength drains away. There could've very easily been two bodies in our yard.

"I didn't see the person or persons or anything, but as I was standing up, I looked to my left and saw the back of the car leaving. There was one of those white, oval stickers with the letters 'SI.' You know what I'm talking about, don't you?"

My hand is clamped over my mouth, but Craig answers her.

"Yes, we know. We know what you're talking about."

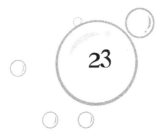

# 23

"Do you think we did the right thing?" I ask Craig over our coffee Monday morning.

"No. But it made the most sense at the time." He sighs and rubs his eyes. "Now to make sure Galena keeps her promise."

I squirm and look at my phone. "Trusting her is absolutely not the right thing, but I so don't want to be in the middle of another police investigation."

"You know we have to tell them she came to us last night."

"At some point. Hopefully after they are too distracted to be mad at us."

Galena realized last night that we were already setting the stage to call the police then and there after she told us about the Sophia Island sticker. She jumped up and plowed to the front door before we knew what was happening.

On the front porch I grabbed her arm. "You could be in danger. You have to tell the police."

"How can I be in danger? No one knows. I'll only be in danger if you tell anyone it was me! Tell them it was an anonymous tip. No one can know I was involved in any of this." She grabbed my arm. "Fiona will be furious!" Then she began pulling my hand off her, peeling my fingers back. I don't think she realized Craig had placed himself between her and the stairs.

"Galena," he said calmly. "The police have to know it was you. They have to find out who did this, and you are their only lead. You don't think Fiona is going to take the fall for any of this, do you? The police are determined to get to the bottom of the pranks, and when they talk to her, do you think she'll take the blame?"

As he spoke, she quit clawing at my hand and leaned on me, almost counting on me to hold her up. Suddenly, as though she realized how weak she looked, she straightened up, gave me a dirty look for touching her, and smiled at Craig.

"You don't know Fiona. We've been best friends for nearly fifty years. If you let me go peaceably, I'll talk to Frank, and we'll go to the police station in the morning." She scoffed at me, actually curling her lip. "It must've been all the pain medicine I took this weekend to think you could, or would, help me."

Craig motioned for me to let go of her, and he stepped out of her way. "Okay. Go talk to Frank and be at the police station at eight a.m. tomorrow. I'm sure we'll hear from them after they talk to you, but if we don't"—he leaned toward her—"we will be down there by nine and tell them everything you said. Plus, I do believe my phone might've been recording your story earlier." He pulled his phone out of his pants pocket, and she gawked at it, like it was a Walmart receipt found in her designer purse. Then she ran down our stairs and onto the sidewalk. Near the road, as the flamingos loomed in front of her, she widened her path and actually ran all the way to the corner.

Now, in the misty sunshine, I look around our still clean and decorated house. This is like doing life in a department store window. "Let's go to Sophia

Coffee, see Eden, and get some kind of a treat for breakfast. The police can find us there just as easily," I say with a wink. "And you're sure you weren't recording last night? It was a good bluff. I mean, I believed you."

He rubs my arm. "You were just hoping. I wish I'd thought of it earlier, before we were standing on the porch. Oh, well. If it scared her, then it's worth it." He stands. "Let's drive so we can go straight from there to the police station."

"If they don't find us first."

"They sell them. There by the cash register." I point, and he sees the white, oval stickers with the black trim and the letters 'SI' in the middle. Below the letters, in tiny print, the car decals say 'Sophia Island.' Along with our small coffees I have a gingerbread scone, and Craig has an icing-covered cinnamon roll. Eden spotted us when we came in, but she was busy in the back.

"I hate to do this, but I'm leaving my phone on the table," I say. "I just can't wait to find out what's going on."

"Did you notice how many cars have

those stickers?" He leans back and tilts his head at me. "I'm kind of surprised you don't have one on yours."

"Don't you mean you're glad I don't have one?" I say as Eden comes up to us. "Hey there. How's the morning going?"

"Pretty quiet so far. What are you two doing out and about so early?"

"I needed a scone and to get out of the house. It's warm outside this morning."

She pulls a chair over from another table. "So I assume you walked over?"

"Walked?" I repeat. "Well, uh—"

She folds her arms on the table and tips her head forward, her rich, brown-ish-red hair falling forward as she lowers her voice. "Something was happening last night, wasn't it? Aiden told me about your 'neighborhood cat.' We don't have a neighborhood cat near the property. He then drove by your house and saw the two of you hurrying back inside. Late. So give. What's going on?"

I smack Craig's knee. "I told you that car slowed down."

"Whatever," Craig says, but he shakes his head at me in warning.

I sigh and say, "We really can't say yet. But come over this afternoon. We can sit out… Oh, no, we can't. The furniture is all going back. Our outdoor stuff too."

"Really?" she says. "Well, that stinks. I was already making up the ads about having an outdoor space for cooler weather."

Craig checks his watch. "At least now we know what that outdoor area can look like. You ready to go?"

Eden shakes her head at us. "Leaving me out in the cold again. Oh, well. I will definitely stop by after my shift, around eleven." We all stand, and she puts her chair back at the other table. "And if there are any gingerbread scones left, I'll bring you another one."

We walk back through the coffee shop. It's nice how slow everything feels this time of year. Downtown was busy this weekend, but during the week it is mostly just us locals. I never thought I'd enjoy a tourist town so much, but it's a whole new way of life. A whole new rhythm.

"There it is." Craig holds up his ringing phone as he gets ready to pull out of our parking space. When he answers, it connects to the car's sound system. "Hello, Daniel. We're heading—"

"I don't care where you're headed. Stay

home. A couple officers are on their way there now."

Craig grimaces at me. "So I take it you've talked to Galena Bellington?"

"Who?"

"Uh, the woman who came in this morning about seeing, um, well, Jasmine getting dropped off at our house."

"I have no idea what you're talking about. We are headed to the prison. Got a call from Charlie Greyson saying he needed to see me and Johnson right away. What do you mean this woman saw Jasmine being dropped off? You mean like after she was dead?"

We both cringe as Craig says, "Yes."

There's a long pause, and just when I'm about to try and explain, he comes back on the phone. "Go home. I'll call you. Don't—*please*—don't talk to anyone else. I know I encouraged your help, but let us handle this right now."

"Okay," we both say solemnly.

I add, "We promise."

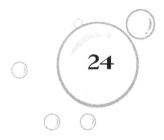

# 24

"This is your idea of not talking to anyone else?" Daniel Ruiz says, stalking into our house around noon. "Is there anyone else we should call to come over? Should I have brought lunch?"

Marisol looks up from her chair and motions for him to take the one placed next to her. "Chill out, detective. They've not said a word. Craig and Jewel only let us in because they took pity on us all sitting on the front porch all morning. And lunch is on its way. We waited to order until we heard you had left the prison."

He motions at young officer Ty Cartle who's been here since we got home. "They heard that from you, I suppose."

"Well, you did call on my radio, and

it's pretty loud." Ty has refused to take a seat and is standing by the front door.

Daniel shakes his head and says to the young man, "Go. Your shift is over, right? Unless you ordered something for lunch."

"Oh, no, sir. I did not. Not to say they didn't try. All nice people, but no, uh, no, sir. No lunch. I'll go now." Ty gives me a little tip of his cap. Poor thing. He tried to be professional, but it's hard with this group.

When the door closes, the detective turns to face the group. "So, wife, what brings you here?"

Marisol lifts a hand toward the backyard. "I made plans to be here overseeing the furniture pickup. We decided at yesterday's committee meeting that we didn't want it to only be the homeowner and the furniture store at the removals, so we committee members spread out. I volunteered to come here."

"Of course you did. Mrs. Bryant?"

Annie frowns at him. "Annie. Everyone calls me Annie, and well, I heard about the 'cat on the porch' incident last night from Aiden. I came over to find out more this morning. Brought some cinnamon rolls if you want one. Or you can just wait for lunch."

His agitation shows, from his tight jaw to the clinched hands on his waist and the way one foot is tapping furiously up and down. "I'm sure everyone has a legitimate reason for being here, correct?"

Hert, never one to answer with just a nod, spouts, "The police scanner alerted me that something was going on at the prison and two Sophia Island police were headed there. We put two and two together, and voilà! Four!" He grins and folds his arms.

Lucy and Cherry just nod and sip their waters.

Eden looks torn; this is her husband's boss after all. Her smile is weak. "I was actually invited to come over after my shift when they stopped in at Sophia Coffee this morning."

Daniel closes his eyes for a moment, then focuses on Craig and me when he opens them. "Okay. Do you want to tell me about last night with all these people listening? It's your decision."

Craig's shrug is dramatic, and he does not look my direction. "Apparently that *is* what we want to do. Whether some of us think it's a good idea or not."

"Ignore him," I say. "It'll save time if we only have to tell it once. Besides, how rude would it be not to include them? They've all waited so long. But first, what did Charlie want?"

Daniel's shoulders relax as much as they can with the thick vest he wears under his uniform. "Hell, everyone probably already knows with the circus out there this morning. Fiona Greyson went out there this morning way before visiting hours, demanding to see her husband. She caused one righteous scene."

"Was there anyone with her?" I ask.

"Now that you mention it, there was someone. A name I hadn't heard until earlier this morning when *you* asked me if I'd talked to her. Galena Bellington."

Gasps of surprise around the room confirm that Craig and I haven't opened our mouths. I look to my right. "Oh, Craig, she didn't go home and talk to Frank! She talked to Fiona. Of course. Why didn't we think of that? After all, they're the ones who are partners in crime." I moan. "So were they allowed to talk to Charlie? What in the world did Fiona think he could do?"

Ruiz frowns before responding. "Keep her friend out of trouble? I think that was the gist of what she was saying."

Marisol lifts a hand. "As in the Bellington Manor Inn? That Galena? She's so, uh, so prissy. I went to a cocktail party there a couple weeks ago, back before we let folks know we were actually a couple, so they didn't know I was associated with the police. Are you saying her blonde friend Fiona is the Fiona that Charlie Greyson is married to? I never imagined! Are you kidding me? I knew he was married, but to her?" Her stricken face gains Marisol lots of points with this group.

Cherry claps her hands to get us back on track. "But what did they have to tell Charlie so badly?"

I announce, "That they are the pranksters!"

Everyone is shocked, then mad. The emotions swirling around the room are like watching one of those crowds do the wave at a football game. The noise level flows up and down as well. Everyone has something to say.

Eden stands and paces for minute before sitting back down. "You mean they cut up all those beautiful poinsettias?"

"Yep," Craig says, and I vigorously nod. "They sure did."

Then Daniel clears his throat. "Maybe not. We don't have an exact list of which pranks were claimed. But you keep saying 'they'?"

I answer for us. "Well, we know Galena and Fiona, and from what Galena said last night, there were some other of their friends involved."

Everything quiets at the detective's look of confusion. His eyes search out mine and Craig's, looking for something, but I have no idea what. After a lengthy pause, he takes out his notebook. "So, what exactly were you told last night?"

Craig and I share the whole experience about someone being on the porch, Aiden showing up, and everything Galena said. Everything all the way to her seeing the murderer flee the scene.

The room is quiet when Tamela whispers, "But I thought the murderer was some gangster from Long Island."

"*Rhode* Island," a couple of us correct her.

Annie raises her hand. Her voice is low and scared. "I have one of those stickers.

All my kids have them too. I put them in their Christmas stockings last year."

A pounding on the door causes us to scream and jump. "Must be lunch," Lucy says as she gets up and goes to the door.

Instead of our sandwich delivery, though, Aiden is standing in the doorframe. "Um, sir? Sorry, but can you step out here a minute?"

"I'll be right back," Ruiz says as he strides to the door, then pulls it tight behind him.

After opening the door, Lucy had moved to the window seat. Eden hurries to join her there. "What is he doing here?" she asks. "He's not on duty until later. Was he in his uniform?"

"No," Lucy says. "Oh, Fiona is here." She jumps up and pulls Eden back to us. "They're coming in!"

I've already stood up, and I remain upright to see what in the world Fiona Greyson could be doing here. Daniel opens the door and starts to say something, but before he can, Fiona rushes inside and straight at me. She throws her arms around me.

"Oh, Jewel! You poor thing. I am so ashamed at how you've been terrorized!"

She takes a quick step back, then launches herself at Craig who is beside me now. She lays her head on his chest for a moment, then steps back again. Tears stream down her face—her fully made-up face. Didn't Daniel say she was at the prison, which is a good hour's drive away, and before visiting hours? She's wearing well-fitting jeans and a soft green sweater with a loose cowl neck. All I can do is blink at her, a reaction that seems to speak for everyone in the room.

She stands there, actually wringing her hands. "Oh, how wretched this all is. When I found out, I had to do everything I could think of to make it all right. How could Galena be so cruel? I thought I knew her. My best friend! Oh, Jewel, how could she do all this to you?" She clutches my upper arms in her cold hands. "But don't worry. Charlie says he'll be sure she's held accountable."

Finally I find my words. Well, maybe just one word, but it explodes from the bottom of my toes. "What?!"

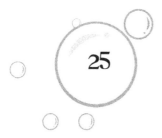

## 25

"Officer Bryant, can you take everyone here outside? Time to go home, folks." Ruiz picks up his wife's purse and hands it to her. "Yes, you too. You can figure out getting your lunch delivered somewhere else."

"Can I get some water?" Fiona asks, and Craig heads off to the kitchen.

I move backward to sit down again, in a seat completely across the room from Fiona Greyson. From everything she just said, she's crazy. She's going to pin all the pranks on Galena. She didn't go out to see Charlie to help her friend—she did it to bury her friend.

Once everyone is outside and the door is closed, Daniel strides my direction. He stands in front of me, blocking my view of the evil blonde in the sweet mint-green sweater. When my mouth opens, he gives me a warning look, then mumbles, "Let her talk."

He intercepts Craig with her water, and I think says the same thing to him because Craig's lips are pressed tight as he takes his seat beside me. Daniel sits, too, a little closer to Fiona than us, and he lets out a long breath. "There. That's better without so many people. Now, Mrs. Greyson, what were you saying?"

"Oh, Daniel, you can call me Fiona. I know you and Charlie go way back. It was so comforting to see you coming in that awful place this morning. With Charlie gone, it's good to know you're here."

He only nods, and there's nothing coming from us, so she takes an awkward sip of water before continuing. "I had to come see you straight away, Jewel. When Galena told me she came to see you last night, I couldn't imagine what for. Then she told me what she's been doing! I was shocked!" Her cheeks color, and tears spring to her eyes again. Her lips are shiny, possibly from some expensive lip gloss, but most likely because she keeps licking them. Then with a little sob she says, "It's all my fault, I'm sure."

Craig immediately puts a hand on my thigh. He knows I want to vehemently agree with her. But he's right. I stay quiet.

She looks from me to Craig, and sadness fills her face. "I had the silliest notion there was something between your wife and my husband. Charlie and I have always had something so special, and when I saw him spending so much time over here, then found out you were out of town all the time, well…" She lifts her hands in a gesture of helplessness. So sweet. So innocent.

"So, in my jealousy, I must've said something about that to my poor friend, and she decided to act in my behalf." Another sob comes out. "Oh, when I think of how frightened you both must've been!"

Daniel turns toward her just a bit. "So, when did you find out what Galena had been doing?"

Her eyes pop wide. "Just last night. She came to unburden herself. She begged me to keep her secret, but I, well, detective, you understand. All these years married to an officer of the law, I just couldn't turn a blind eye." She looks down, then up through her lashes. "I know. I should've called you immediately, but all I could think to do was talk to Charlie." Then she breaks down completely, though she somehow manages to get out, "I miss him so much. He was my rock."

We wait on her to regain her composure while I repeat the Pledge of Allegiance to myself to keep from flying out of this chair and strangling her. Every word is a lie. The pledge and the calming looks from both Craig and Daniel keep me sitting and mute.

Ruiz patiently asks, "So, Mrs. Greyson, what did Mrs. Bellington tell you about the night of the flamingo prank?"

"First, can you imagine anything so tacky?" She sniffs, then chuckles. "That alone testifies that I could have had nothing to do with this." When we don't laugh with her, she continues. "So she said she put them on the lawn, then something about gluing on those awful hats." She studies each of us. "That's when that body was dumped here? And there was a car here too?"

None of us verify either matter, so she shrugs. "But you should know—now, I'd never say this under any other circumstances, but she's addicted to her 'headache pills,' as she calls them. They completely knock her out. Her poor husband has to do everything at the inn because she's so often drugged." She looks at Craig. "Did she seem rational to you last night? She was all over the place, frantic, wasn't she?" Taking in a deep breath, she shakes her head, then stands. "She's been this way for months. I know now I should not have talked so open and honestly with her. She just wasn't stable. But now it's all behind us. I'm sure Frank will get her the help she needs."

She places a thin, perfectly manicured hand on Detective Ruiz's shoulder and squeezes. "Could you please give me a ride home, Daniel? I don't feel strong enough to drive. Maybe one of your officers can bring my car to my house."

"Of course, Mrs. Greyson." He stands but looks at the two of us left behind and raises a finger once her back is turned. We follow them to the door, then do as instructed and wait.

He sticks his head back inside. "Thanks for just listening. I wanted to get that all on the record. We'll talk later."

Then it's just us. In our empty house.

The craziness has all been pushed out there—beyond that thick, heavy door.

I fall into Craig's arms, and we stand like that, holding each other up for several minutes. When I look at him, my hand reaches up to caress the nape of his neck. Then, gently pressing, my fingers encourage his head to dip, encourage his lips to meet mine. Suddenly we're in the middle of a kiss that needs to resolve in more than a makeout session on the couch. He pulls away to flip the lock on the front door. Then, taking my hand, he walks across the living room, down the back hall, and to the door of his room. He pauses as if to lean in for a kiss, but I don't pause with him. I push open the door and pull him inside with me.

"Close the door," I breathe. "I don't want to hear the phones if they ring."

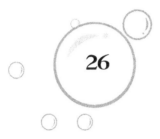

**26**

"So, where were you this afternoon?" Annie asks as soon as I answer the phone, not giving me a chance to answer. "When I brought y'all's sandwiches by, Craig said you were taking a nap, but I could clearly see your bedroom door upstairs was open. So be honest. Did you go out to the prison and see Charlie?"

That takes the smile off my face. "No! I didn't go see Charlie. Why? What's happening?" Just like that, my bubble is burst. I get up from the couch to talk in the little bathroom downstairs. Craig is in the kitchen making us hot chocolate; there's no need for his bubble to be burst too.

"Charlie is as Charlie has been since high school. He apparently believes she had nothing to do with the pranks." She hesitates. "And, well, I might've heard that he wants to talk to you."

"No. There's no need for that. The home tour is over, my kids are all coming in this weekend, and I'm not getting caught up in more of the Charlie–Fiona drama. This has nothing to do with me."

"Well, Jasmine was left in *your* yard in the middle of one of her pranks."

"By some out-of-state gangster. Craig googled Providence, and it's a hotbed of corruption. He figures they sent some low-level crook down here to get the thumb drive, and somehow she was killed. It could've just been coincidence that she was left in our yard. Maybe the flamingos looked like a good distraction for a murder."

"Really? What about the Sophia Island sticker on the getaway car?"

I blow out a breath and sit down on the closed toilet lid. "Maybe she imagined it? I'm not agreeing with Fiona, but Galena was pretty erratic. Maybe she's mistaken, but…"

"Exactly! *But…*" After a momentary silence, she adds, "So you aren't going to talk to Charlie?"

"No."

"Think I should?"

"If you want. Yeah, take Aiden with you. See what he has to say."

She thinks for a bit. "Okay. I think I will. And maybe I can help him see his lovely bride for the lunatic she is."

She's quiet again.

"Are you thinking or what? I have hot chocolate waiting. "

"Uh, do you want to know where Lucy is?"

"What? What do you mean? Where is she?"

"She went to see Galena."

"Oh, really? But they do run in some of the same circles, so it makes sense, I guess. Wonder if Galena knows Fiona threw her under the bus?"

"Oh, she knows. According to Aiden, Fiona left her stranded at the prison this morning. She had to call Frank to come bring her home, and he was not happy. Apparently he was at the Jacksonville airport, and he missed his flight."

"You'd think he'd be more concerned with his wife having a breakdown. Not to mention being the witness in a murder—well, part of a murder." I hear Craig tell me my hot chocolate is getting cold. "Hey,

I've got to go. Thanks for the update. Keep me in the loop."

"Sure, hon. Bye."

I can't help but grin. Annie was so preoccupied she didn't even come close to guessing where I spent my afternoon.

"Yum. That smells good. Thanks." Christmas mugs on the coffee table look appealing, but not as appealing as my husband sitting there in the shorts and T-shirt he's had on since our 'nap.'

He pulls down a soft blanket from the back of the couch. "Come on. I've got you a spot right here. All snug and warm."

I settle in beside him, keeping it to a short kiss since we do have hot chocolate waiting. "The blanket feels good; it must be getting colder out."

As we clink our mugs in a toast, he laughs. "Well, not exactly. Matter of fact, it's pretty warm. So, in order to snuggle with you, I turned the air conditioner on!"

After our hot chocolate, I settle in for some major online shopping. Craig went for a short run, so I decide to multitask and call Lucy to see how her visit with Galena went while I shop.

"Frank wouldn't let me in," she says. "I'm on my way home now. He said she was resting."

"Pshaw. I hope what she's doing is re-evaluating her friends. Although anyone who trusts Fiona Greyson gets what they deserve."

"That goes double for Charlie. Annie said she's going out to see him first thing in the morning. I'm ready to wash my hands of the whole thing. I have Christmas parties and get-togethers pretty much solid from now to kingdom come." Her voice thickens. "In the past Mother would come with me. She'd get all gussied up, and everyone would dote on her. Now I have to do it all alone. No Birdie. No Davis." Lucy never feels sorry for herself, and the sadness in her voice now is so hard to hear.

I look up from my Amazon shopping cart, focused fully on my friend. "Oh, I know it's been hard," I say sympathetically. "And Birdie just breaks my heart. It's awful to see her slowing down, and I've only known her a short while. I can't imagine how it is for you."

"She's always been the life of the party." Her voice trails off, but then she clears her throat. "Maybe it's time for me to slow down too. Stay home with her more. Davis loved getting all dressed up and going out. We were a good match in that department. But I know, I know. He's scum, and I'm glad I know who he really is. It's hard to go out, too, because I worry what he's telling people about me."

"No one believes him. People know you too well for that. Tell you what, I'd love to spend some time with Birdie. You just let me know when there's a party you want to go to, and I'll come visit with her."

"Aww, Jewel, she'd love that!" Lucy enthuses. "But it's really okay. I should have y'all out here for dinner this week. It's going to stay warm all week, and the deck is so nice. How about tomorrow night?"

"The ladies, or me and Craig? I'm good with either."

"Everybody! Let's get everyone together. Mother will be so excited to see everyone." Now her excitement sounds a little overwrought. Lucy is someone we've never had to worry about, but things seem to really be piling up on her.

"Are you sure? It seems like a lot for you and Birdie. Wait, I know! My daughter was telling me something she and her friends have done. Everyone brings take-out food to share. It's easy and fun to sample everything."

Lucy laughs. "That sounds perfect and low-maintenance! I'll send out a group text when I get home." She takes in a breath and exhales. "Oh, thank you, Jewel. I feel so much better. I was feeling sorry for myself, and, you know, I'm just not good at that!"

"You've had a rough fall, but everything is going to get better from here on out."

We say goodbye, and I start to hang up when she yells my name.

"I'm still here."

"Should I invite Marisol and Daniel?"

"My first reaction is yes, but it's up to you."

"My first reaction is yes too. Okay, good. Plus, we can get an update on what's going on in the investigations!"

We hang up this time, and I look around our brightly lit house. Life is so crazy. How many nights have I sat in this chair, lonely, afraid of the future, envying Lucy and her easy relationship with Davis? Now we all know why it was so easy; no commitment meant he could have his cake and eat it too. No one would ever say my relationship with Craig is easy. For the last several years it's been anything but, from his constant traveling to me dealing with an empty nest, to this move falling on us like a ton of bricks. But I look at us now, and I'm glad we struggled through.

Easy is overrated.

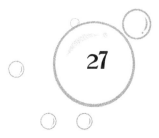

**27**

"Want to ride out to Shug Miller's house in the morning?" Craig asks as he comes into the kitchen. His hair is damp from the shower he took after his run.

"Let me guess," I say with a sigh. "She didn't hand over her furniture willingly this afternoon." We'd been so preoccupied when the truck and movers showed up here that our backyard and front porch were bare before we knew it. My face flushes thinking of the texts from Marisol saying she was there with the furniture movers but didn't know where we were. When we were there—just ignoring everything but each other.

"You got it. There was no one home, and she wasn't answering her phone all day. I've worked out a deal with the store owner, which I've emailed to her. I want to go personally to get her answer. She finally just responded to my text and says she'll be there but makes no promises. I did attach a letter laying out the penalty fees if she doesn't let the furniture go back tomorrow." He lays his chin on my shoulder as he passes. "I guess it's good all our things to go back were outside and easily accessible." He kisses my warm cheek and I give him a pat on his backside as he goes by.

"Yeah, I'll go. I'm always up for a drive down the island; plus it should be entertaining. She's a real pistol." I fix some bunched-up greenery in the window and recenter the battery-powered candle. "Wonder what Jasmine thought when she went out to Shug's house and realized she knew who she really was? Are you surprised Jasmine didn't leave town then?"

He sits in a kitchen chair. "Sort of, but it sounds like Shug needed Jasmine too. They both seem to play fast and loose with the rules. Shug was more than willing to scratch Jasmine's back if she got hers scratched. That must've been enough for her to not feel threatened."

"And yet she should have."

He nods.

I start the dishwasher and turn out the overhead light. Now the room is lit only by the twinkle lights on the porch and the ones lining the cabinet tops.

"Can you get the colored lights out of the closet tonight so we don't forget to put them on the living room tree before Carver and Ellie get here?" I ask. "It's going to be so fun celebrating Christmas with little ones again."

"I'll get them out right now," Craig says as he stands, then follows me out of the kitchen. "Do you want to watch something? We have a long list of Christmas movies to get in this month."

"No, we have to save those for when the kids are here."

"You're so cute," he says, hugging me from behind, his head on my shoulder as he looks at the tree.

I turn in his arms. "I know what I want to do."

"Oh, Mrs. Mantelle! After this afternoon and then running, I don't know." He laughs and squeezes me. "But I can try. Trying is fun."

"Not that, but it is something that will be tiring."

He frowns. "Okay, now what."

I meet his eyes. "Let's move you into our bedroom upstairs."

He catches his breath, and I'm shocked when tears swim in his eyes. "Really?"

All I manage is a quick nod before I bury my face in his chest.

Really.

"I hear you're going to be the chairman for next year's tour. We need to talk about that before I make any concessions on my furniture."

Shug is, as Annie would say, loaded for bear when she opens her huge, glass front door and hits us with both barrels.

"No," Craig says. Then he turns to look at my shocked face. "No, I'm definitely not going to be the chairman. Believe me, the museum people have learned their lesson the hard way. All future chairmen will be thoroughly vetted, so I have absolutely no power or control over their decision. I just want to get this year wrapped up and forget I've ever heard the words 'Christmas Home Tour.' What a cool house!" He deftly moves past Shug and into the large, open room. "I hear your living room furniture is eggplant in color. I can see how that would really bring this all together. Such a dramatic backdrop with all the windows!"

I poke him in his back as I catch up with him. Who is this guy? I guess he watched HGTV when he was living in South Florida. He continues on his decorator tour. "And what's this called, where the living room is a step down?"

Shug is right on our heels. "Sunken. A sunken living room. But I've grown tired of all this. I'm so ready for my New England house. You should see it: steep roof, gable windows, designer wallpaper in every room. And none of this 'authentic' Christmas crap Pam insisted on. I like the tinsel and colored lights and Santa Claus red. Our real house at home will be a real Santa's workshop by this weekend!"

"Oh, that's right," I say. "You're headed to Rhode Island soon, right?"

She clouds up. "Not soon enough for me. That friend of yours who brought her husband the other day, you know, the mousy girl? Well, he's got Donald interested in some model railroad show that's going to be up in Georgia, so we're hanging around for that."

Craig doesn't need to ask who she's

talking about. He smiles at me, then turns his attention back to our hostess, who is now seated in the very middle of the cream leather sectional, her arms spread out across the back. The pillows I liked are all gone, as are a lot of the decorations. It was a collaboration between the professional decorators and the homeowners, and some, like us, bought a lot of the items at a steep discount. Since we're running an event business in our home and had never decorated the Mantelle Mansion for Christmas, it made sense for us. But it appears even the flocked trees are gone. I'd assumed those belonged to the Millers. Could retro Christmas decorations be a real thing for real interior designers?

"So, the furniture?" Craig steers the conversation back to his main concern.

She looks at it, rubs her hand on the soft leather, and sighs. "I love it. Truly do. It would be beautiful in Donny's house up home, but he says he doesn't want it. They like the furniture they have." She sits up and shudders. "Uncomfortable! Let me tell you. It's like sitting in an art gallery or something. What is it with young people these days?"

I stop in my examination of what's

left from the tour decorations. "Wait, you were going to ship *this* to New England?"

"No, that would cost an arm and a leg. We'd rent a truck and drive it. I don't like to fly, and we have so much to take that we always drive. It was going to be our Christmas gift to them, but nooo." She rolls her eyes in general disgust. "His wife thinks being comfortable is the same as being ugly. You should see those heels she wears."

Shug pushes herself up from the couch. "You should've seen Donny spread out on this, legs up, head back watching football. Of course in the princess's house the televisions are only in the bedrooms and the basement. Donny gets no say-so whatsoever on what he wants. And he's the one paying all those bills. And she sure does know how to ring up some bills. Of course, with the family she was raised in…" She lets it hang, but we have no doubt of her opinion of her daughter-in-law and her family.

Craig puts his phone back in his pocket and announces, "The furniture truck is on its way. They're going to take this one out and will put yours back in place. It's on the truck from yesterday."

"Okay," Shug says, looking like she's

trying to remember actually telling him she's returning it. Then she abruptly stands. "Well, I'll let you people get on your way," she dismisses us as she power-walks to the front door. "And you're not lying about not being chairman next year, are you? Can't believe I've lost all my leverage."

"No, I'm not lying. But thanks for asking," Craig says with a wink at me as we hurry across the terra-cotta foyer behind her.

"Have a good trip back home, and drive safe," I say, reaching out to shake her extended hand after I first opened my arms to give her a hug.

She scrunches her nose and pulls open the heavy door. "I don't go for all that hugging they do down here. Whew! Feel that heat. I don't like that either. I don't know. I might just sell this house and stay back home. It sounded like an adventure when we bought this house, but I think the condo at the resort would be more than fine for Donald's business meetings."

I stop and turn. "Jasmine—I mean Pam—had a condo here along with her townhome downtown. I'm surprised how many people do. You know, live here but have a place at the resort too."

"They were probably like us: bought a condo to try out living down here, then just kept it. It makes it nice for when you have company or just need a weekend on the beach. Or they could even rent it out."

Me staring at her just a bit too long makes Shug frown and demand, "What?"

I shake my head and smile. "Nothing. Just daydreaming for a minute. That does sounds nice, just getting away to the beach any time you feel like it."

She doesn't say anything, just gives me a quick nod, then steps back inside and closes the glass door.

Craig waits by the van, holding my door open. "What was all that about?"

I frown at him, then get in. He goes around the van and gets in too. We pull out of the paver-stone driveway and pass the luxury golf-course homes as we head to A1A. When he puts his blinker on to turn left, I put my hand on his arm.

"Want to go take a ride through Island Resort?"

He smiles and switches the direction of his blinker. "Of course, Mrs. Mantelle. Lead the way."

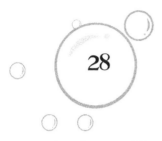

# 28

"I was very clear there would be no home-made dishes allowed," Lucy explains. "Mother was perturbed at first. She said she'd never heard of anything so rude. But her moods come and go fast these days, so she got over it. Now she's obsessed with making sure no one breaks the rules."

I point out back toward the deck over-looking the ocean. "She seems to be enjoying her role as gatekeeper out there. She's making everyone show her what they brought. I didn't realize Craig had never met her since he moved back here. She's telling him stories of how everyone couldn't believe he would come stay in the summers with his great-aunt Cora and how even with him here, his aunt still stayed in the house all the time."

Lucy pulls out some big serving spoons from a drawer and hands them to me. "Put these on the table. Is everyone here? I'd love to hear what memories Craig has of Sophia Island back then. Does he ever talk about it?"

"Some, but he's not big on memories. Our counselor says it doesn't seem like he's holding anything back, just doesn't remember. He says some people are like that. And I do think everyone is here. Can I carry anything else to the table?"

Annie and Ray are taking the tops off the different food items as I lay the spoons down.

"This is such a great idea. I might suggest this for the next family gathering," Annie says.

Ray shakes his head at her. "No, you won't. You won't even allow something other than marshmallows to go on top of your sacred sweet potatoes. I'm still scalded from when I used walnuts instead of pecans in a pan of brownies from a box."

She opens her mouth to argue, then closes it. "Yeah, you might be right. It's all ready," she announces to the group.

Lucy steps toward the screen door between us and our friends outside. "Time to eat. Just eat wherever you can find a place to sit. Someone want to say grace?"

I'm not the only one who is surprised when Craig raises his hand and volunteers as we all gather around the table. "Lord, we want to say thank you for this food and the people here. Thank you for the memories you've allowed me to share with Miss Birdie and for bringing me, along with Jewel, back here. Amen."

Daniel Ruiz speaks up as he puts his arm around his wife. "We appreciate being invited. It's time folks got to know us as a couple."

From chicken wings to steamed dumplings to hush puppies to a veggie platter, the food is varied and delicious. We also decided to stick with only tea, soda, beer, or wine. No fancy margaritas like we tend to have when the ladies do lunch here.

Birdie asked to eat outside, so once we get her set up out there, everyone else finds a seat. I find myself with Marisol, Annie, and Lucy at the small inside dining table. "We so appreciate you and Ray bringing our front porch furniture over this afternoon," I tell Annie. "This weather is perfect for sitting outside."

"No problem. I should've texted you

we were coming, but we ended up going by your place sooner than I thought. Where were y'all off to?"

"We went to Shug's to make sure she turned in her living room set and then took a ride out to the resort. Ended up having lunch there. Did y'all know Shug and her husband have a condo on the resort? We found out it's actually in the same complex as the one Jasmine and her husband own."

Annie's eyes go large before she squints. "That's a little too much of a coincidence for me. They knew each other back up north, and then they bought condos in the same complex? I mean, that place is huge. What's the chances?"

Marisol lowers her voice. "Daniel may be wanting to tell you all this himself, but"—she pauses for effect—"it might not be a coincidence."

"I knew it!" I say under my breath.

Marisol grins. "Jewel called Daniel from the resort, and he was out there just before we came here. That's why we drove separately. The Millers and the Fergusons, both from Providence, Rhode Island, bought their condos within weeks of each other. And remember those meetings you talked about Jasmine's husband holding?"

Lucy asks, "Same with Donald Miller?"

"Yep."

"Shoot," I say. "I should've checked the Millers' cars to see if they have one of those Sophia Island stickers. Maybe Shug's husband is involved in Jasmine's death. Craig and I can drive over there when we leave here."

Annie shakes her head at me. "No. You don't need to be messing around over there. Let the police decide if there's anything more to it. It may be as simple as a real estate agent working that area. I really can't believe Donald would have anything to do with this. You met him. Can't say boo to an ant. Now Shug? Oh, sweetie, you don't want to mess with Shug Miller."

Marisol laughs her agreement. "Yes, they are looking into a connection, and Sergeant Johnson is pushing for more information from Rhode Island police." She lowers her voice. "Between us, I think the police were so happy to have the case solved, they ignored some pieces that didn't fit. But just for a bit. Let's see what they find out."

"Sorry to interrupt y'all in here, but

where's the dessert table?" Martin Berry asks. "Miss Birdie has sent me in to bring her some of whatever sweet there is. Of course I don't want her to have to eat it alone, so…"

"Here you go," Lucy says, getting up. "They're in the kitchen."

Annie whispers to me and Marisol, "I'm glad Martin is here, and of course I'm happy Ray was invited, but I want to talk all this murder stuff out!" Her brow is pressed low and her jaw set. "I haven't gotten to tell anyone what Charlie had to say this morning, and I'm about to bust."

"Charlie Greyson?" Marisol asks. "You went to see him? What did he say about that wife of his? She's really a piece of work." In a flash Marisol has gone from laughing to full-on angry. "That woman is calling and texting Daniel at all hours." She takes on a whimpering, wispy woman's voice. "She's scared. She doesn't trust the other officers. Can you come check my windows?" Marisol's dark eyes are hard, black, and there's red in her cheeks. "I went with him last night, and she was there in a nightie I wouldn't wear on my honeymoon. Waiting on *my* husband!"

Annie and I have drawn in surprised

breaths at the sudden outburst, but then Annie slaps the table. "Woo-wee! You are one ferocious lady about your man. I like that! Good move going with him. She's always catting around for good-looking men. Did you lay into her?" Her eyes are sparkling. Marisol has gained a big fan; Annie can't stand Fiona Greyson.

"No," Marisol breathes out. "Daniel wouldn't even let me get out of the car."

"Well, can you blame him?" I give her a sly look. "He's already got one murder to investigate."

A loud clap of thunder causes us all to jump, and then those on the deck come pushing inside the room. There is wind blowing rain in with them, and by the time they get Birdie inside they are all wet.

"I told you it was going to rain," Birdie says over and over.

"Yes, ma'am, you did," Hert agrees. "We just didn't move fast enough."

"Annie, Jewel, grab some towels out of the bathroom for them. I'll get Mother dried off in her room," Lucy says as everyone scurries around. The beach house isn't very big, especially not when we have a table of food set up in the middle of it, but this gets everyone cleaning up faster than usual.

By the time Lucy comes back out, the table is put away, and we're all situated on the floor or in chairs, leaving Miss Birdie's chair empty for her.

"Mother's ready for bed," Lucy says. "She said to tell everyone she had a wonderful time and that she's up for one of these tacky parties anytime. Also, she wants another one of those macarons from Karen's that someone brought."

As Lucy retrieves and delivers the pretty lavender macaron to her mother, Martin laughs. "I haven't moved that fast in years. That thunderclap scared me to death!"

Cherry gives her husband a challenging look. "Now that I've seen how fast you can move, I'm going to get you to start running with me."

He groans. "I don't want to lose weight that bad."

There's a little more chatter as Lucy comes back out and we all finish our desserts. I look around the room, and it's beginning to feel awkward. Then Ray lifts one of his big hands in surrender. "Okay, okay. I know what's going on. All y'all except me and Martin want to talk about your latest mystery. I get it. That's what y'all do. And y'all know why I've been uncomfortable with it since what all happened back in the fall, but I'm giving up. It's not fair to Annie to make her retell everything later to me while at the same time I'm acting like I don't want to know!" His big laugh fills the cozy room.

Annie hits us with an exaggerated 'What can I say' look, but she keeps her mouth closed tight.

Ray gives her a sweet look. "Aww, hon, you can talk now. I wanted to not care about it all and act like I'm beyond all that, but honestly, I wanted to know everything. And I can't stand a hypocrite. So if you want to have a session of the Scooby-Doo team, I'm okay with it."

Craig laughs and sticks his hand out to Ray to shake. "Nice to meet ya, Shaggy here."

Ray shakes his hand, winks, then with a wave of his hand, he puts Martin on the spot. "Sorry brother, but I've gone to the dark side."

Martin is a serious computer guy. He works from home and struggles with his weight. He's probably the husband, except for Daniel Ruiz, I know the least about.

He rubs his mostly bald head and shudders. "I just don't know if I have the stomach or the heart for all this. But let's give it a go." He adds with a weak chuckle, "I'll just go out in the storm if I feel I can't hack it."

Cherry gets up and goes over to him, pulls his arm off the table, and sits on his knee for a minute. Then when she stands, she kisses him on his forehead. "If you want to leave, just give me our high sign and we're out of here."

"Wait," Tamela shouts. "You have a high sign? What is it?"

Martin looks at Cherry and then exaggeratedly mouths, "Let's go!"

We all laugh, and Cherry shakes her head. "Yeah. Subtle we are not."

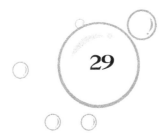

**29**

"You seem quiet," Annie says to me. I walked out on the deck for a breath of fresh air as we wait for Ray and Craig to take the garbage down and help Lucy bring up some Christmas decorations from her storage closet. Annie followed me. Everyone else has left.

The darkness out over the ocean is still now that the storm has passed, and the air is cooler. I wish my mind could quiet down like that. "You said Charlie completely believes Fiona? He actually thinks Fiona's friends were that invested in pestering me that they did all the pranks? She's completely innocent?"

Annie rests her hands on the wet railing. "Yeah. I thought he might be seeing through her this past year, given how he acted towards you, but I think being in prison has made it worse than ever for him. He's hanging on to that marriage and the way the officers were saying she's been out there visiting him and sending him stuff." She throws up her arms. "Maybe she has changed."

I dismiss that with a shake of my head. "Except we *know* she was behind the pranks. Galena came and confessed to us that she was following Fiona's lead. Besides, have you ever considered Galena Bellington to be the ringleader type? Even in her marriage, Frank is definitely the one in charge. That's evident to everybody. Now, maybe Fiona got in too deep with the pranks and just wants to slough it off on Galena? *That* I can buy. But her being completely innocent? No way."

"Well, either way. The pranks are done and over, whoever was behind them. Now to get this mess with Jasmine or Pam or whoever wrapped up so we can continue with our Christmases. When do your kids get here?"

I exhale. "Erin and Sadie are actually on the same flight from Atlanta with their husbands and babies late Thursday night. Both boys get in Friday morning."

"Do we get to meet them? I really want to meet them. I know! Why don't we all meet at Dickens on Centre Friday night? Early, before it gets dark, we can have a drink at Fezziwig's Tavern, which is set up outside at the old train depot welcome center. That way we don't interfere with your family stuff, and you and the kids will get to see what all is happening at the festivities downtown."

"You know, I think that would be perfect. I have no idea where to even start with the Dickens on Centre stuff, and I really didn't have anything planned for Friday in case they're tired. I can see if everyone—"

Annie places a hand on my arm. "I'll let everyone know. You just get your family there. We'll meet at the train depot at the opening. I think it's four, but I'll check. I'd suggest y'all just walk over from your house. Parking isn't impossible, but y'all are so close, and the weather is supposed to be perfect."

We turn as we hear the guys carrying the red and green bins up the stairs. Lucy comes into view first. "Y'all have no idea how grateful I am. I hate lugging those things up those stairs."

"And we expect a call when they have to go back down," Craig says.

Annie and I open the back door, then follow them inside.

Ray sets the red bin in his hands down with a huff. "I was thinking about what Officer Ruiz said tonight, how everyone up in Rhode Island says the murder was done by someone from up there, but I don't know how much we should trust them. I mean, there's already more connections between Providence and our island than I'm comfortable calling coincidence."

I vehemently nod. "But who? Why? Shug is the one who told us everything we know. If she wanted to kill Jasmine, or Pam as she knows her, why would she tell anyone about the connection?"

Annie scoffs. "To throw us off. She's mean, but she's not stupid, though she thinks everyone down here *is*. A bunch of slow-walking, slow-talking morons, that's how she sees us. And apparently, according to Daniel, both of the Millers' cars have the SI stickers. He also said Galena doesn't remember where on the car the sticker was, just that there was one. It's so frustrating! We learned a lot tonight, but it didn't get us anywhere. Maybe Galena doesn't actually remember it correctly and the sticker was for something else! Who knows at this point?"

Craig picks up my purse and hands it to me, which is apparently our high sign that it's time to leave. He says, "And remember, Daniel said the Millers both were accounted for Thursday night until almost eleven at that neighborhood Christmas party. They were on the cleanup committee and actually had to sign off on the sheet at the clubhouse."

I take my purse and sigh. "Yeah, and now that we know the ransacking of Jasmine's townhome was done that evening near ten, they couldn't have done it." We are all a bit discouraged as we go quiet and head to the door.

Lucy chuckles. "That's why I don't have a dog. So I won't be out walking it and witness a crime! But thank goodness Jasmine's neighbor *was* out and about. Now, if only she was more help than just telling us she heard things being thrown about and saw the lights go out. It's good to have a time, but…"

I hug Lucy goodbye. "That's true about late-night dog walking, but thank

God that's all she saw or the dog owner might've ended up on our lawn too."

We get into our cars. Annie and Ray turn south, and then we turn north. We pull out onto quiet, dark streets. Even without the sea turtle regulations on lights at the beach, the farther away from the resort you get, A1A on Sophia Island is a like an old-fashioned beach road. There are Christmas lights on some of the houses, most with a distinctive coastal flair. Palm tree trunks are roped with strings of lights, turquoise instead of green and vibrant pink in place of red, but it's still dark and quiet as we drive north. At the turn to go west toward town and home, Craig turns right, into the parking lot for The Dunes restaurant and Main Beach. There are a few parking spots along the shore, and there are benches placed all along the sidewalk. I often take this little detour to see if a parking spot is open because if there is, it would be a shame not to stop, right?

Tonight there isn't one. "Well, I'm surprised," Craig says. "I felt sure on a Tuesday night in December we'd get lucky."

"But look up there." On the second floor of The Dunes there are lots of lights, and there's an obvious party going on.

"They've renovated the second floor, and although you can't go outside up there, there's a great view of the beach. I bet the main attraction for holding a party up there is their whiskey library. Apparently they have the largest whiskey collection in the state of Florida."

"Really?" Craig says as we pull up to the red light where A1A makes its turn and travels all the way down the east coast of Florida. "Maybe the guys and I should come check it out this weekend."

"Maybe. Annie and I were talking about the weekend, and she suggested we all meet at the old train depot downtown early Friday evening. It becomes Fezziwig's Tavern for Dickens on Centre."

"Oh, Fezziwig like from *A Christmas Carol*. I get it. And I've seen the notices that the downtown streets are closed, so I'm assuming there are lots of vendors and food trucks."

"That's what I hear. Not as many as there were for Shrimp Fest, but enough so we can walk around and eat." I reach over and squeeze his arm. "I can't believe the kids will all be here in just a few days."

"Oh! Wonder what's going on?" Craig says as he turns off of Centre Street and nears our house. As we arrive at our driveway, we can see police lights and cars farther ahead.

"Don't turn in; keep going," I say.

At the corner we stop, and I see the officer blocking traffic is the young man who was with Ty the first day we were under police protection. He's the one that stayed with Craig at the Ponces' house. "Ask him what's going on," I urge.

"Hi," Craig says, rolling down the window.

The officer recognizes him immediately. "Oh, Mr. Mantelle. Hi. This road is closed."

"I see that. What's going on?"

"Can't really say."

I stretch over to see him out Craig's window. "Is there anything we should be worried about?"

He looks back over his shoulder. "I don't think so, but, well, there's been a shooting, ma'am. That's about all I know. I think you should go home, lock the doors, and stay there. I mean, that's what I'd tell my mom." He gives me a crooked smile, then backs away.

"A shooting?" I am already digging out my phone as Craig turns the car around.

"Should I call Annie or Marisol first? It feels almost like a betrayal, but Annie's going to have more questions than answers."

Marisol picks up on the first ring. "Are you home? You're okay?"

"We just pulled up and saw all the cops and lights, but they're on the next street. There's been a shooting!"

"That's about all I know too. You remember Daniel and I drove to Lucy's separately, so I was almost home when Daniel called and said he needed to check something out. Then just a few minutes ago he called and told me not to go out as there'd been a shooting. He said not to worry but that he wouldn't be home for a while. He also told me to call you and tell you and Craig to do the same about staying inside. I was just getting ready to call you. So, what is going on is near your house?"

"Oh, wait, Annie is calling. I'll see if she's heard anything."

"Okay. Call me back."

"Annie?" I answer the other line.

"Oh, Jewel! Aiden says there's been a shooting near you. Are you okay?"

"We're fine. Just got home and we're going inside, locking the doors, and staying there. Did he say anything else?"

"Yeah, he thinks it's at the Bellington Inn." She pauses. "And, Jewel, he says someone's dead."

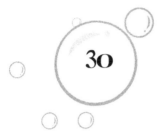

# 30

"Galena Bellington committed suicide," I tell Craig as I sit on the edge of our bed early Wednesday morning. We'd suspected as much by the time we went to bed late last night, but the call from Annie just now confirmed it.

"They're sure it's suicide?"

"She left a note." I stand up and step over to the window. Leaves still cover the live oak trees, which cover our bedroom windows. These leaves won't drop until the new ones push them out in the spring. It makes it feel even less like Christmas, especially with the morning's news.

All evening we'd heard bits and pieces, that just one person was involved and there was no hunt for the perpetrator or the weapon. We knew Frank had been spotted because Tamela and Hert went to check in on his mother, Charlotte, at the police's request. She lives in a cottage on the property. Charlotte is a well-known, crotchety, old woman who scares the living daylights out of most people here, including me. She refused to open the door to someone she didn't know, even if they were the police. One of the officers knew Hert and Tamela were friends of Charlotte—well, as much as that's possible—so they were called. They were only allowed to get the police in the door, not stay to get any information.

Still looking out the window, I tell Craig, "The note apparently says something like Jasmine knew Galena was behind the pranks. So when she caught Jasmine spying on her when she was putting out the flamingos, she killed her."

"What?" Craig sits up in bed. "But that's not right. She wasn't killed here. Right? She died somewhere else."

As I turn toward him, I shrug. "That's what I thought. Annie's coming over. She's been up baking all night, so she's bringing whatever she's made. I'm sure you're welcome to join—"

He cuts me off. "No, you ladies have

the place to yourselves. I'm going to take a walk and end up downtown at the coffee shop. Want to get out and clear my head. I'll be out of here in just a few minutes if you want to take your time waking up and getting dressed."

I smile at him and nod. He gives me a kiss on his way past me, and I sit back down on the bed and pick up my phone. According to the texts I've accumulated in the last few minutes, all the ladies are coming over. We always seem to gather here. At first my house was such an oddity no one had been inside of for years, so they all wanted to meet here. It's also close to downtown. I guess since we're set up for an event space it still makes sense, but I wonder if Craig will get tired of it being the group's unofficial clubhouse?

"She left a video?" We're all shocked by Marisol's news. I look at Annie. "But you said it was a note."

"That's what I was told." She frowns. "Well, maybe I just assumed. A video? Like on her phone?"

Marisol nods. "Yes. I haven't seen it, but I have seen a transcript of it." She looks guiltily around our little circle. We're seated in the living room, Annie, Lucy, Tamela, Cherry, Marisol, and me. Annie brought a loaf of cranberry-orange bread, and we're eating off paper Christmas plates. The mood is anything but festive. "I overheard Daniel on the phone this morning when he came home to shower and put on his uniform. And, well, you know he can't exactly take his phone in the shower. It was just lying there in our room." She shrugs, and the rest of us mimic her guilty look.

But our guilt passes quickly, and Tamela asks, "So, what did it say?"

"Galena wanted to curry favor with Fiona, so she started pranking you. She explicitly said Fiona had nothing to do with the pranks. I don't know if she said how Jasmine found out it was her, but she was holding it over her head, so she had to kill her."

Lucy tuts. "Well, that sounds a tad extreme and doesn't sound like the Galena Bellington I know. She'd just say Jasmine was lying and dare her to prove it. And if she had proof she'd ignore that. I'm just not buying she was that afraid of Jasmine."

Cherry sighs and picks at her piece of

bread. "Except there's a video. How do you fake that? Could she have been coerced? But I'm sure the police are looking into that."

"Don't be so sure of that," Marisol says. "The Rhode Island police were already all over it this morning and closed the case on their end. They went from claiming all responsibility to washing their hands of it completely. And I don't think it will surprise you ladies, but Sergeant Johnson is in full agreement with them. It's all over. The pranks. The murder. Everything. All wrapped up tightly in a nice, authentic red bow!"

"Wait," Annie blurts. "What about Jasmine's townhouse being searched? Galena did that too?"

Marisol closes her eyes and winces. "Random home invasion."

We all react in disgust. Then after I think for a moment, I tip my head at the detective's wife. "I have a feeling that might just be why Daniel felt the need to come home and take a shower. To talk so loud on the phone. *And* to leave his phone out for you. It's also probably why his phone's unlock code is known to you."

She smiles at us. "Could be. He did

say he thought it would be good if I wasn't alone this morning. That it would be good to get together with my new friends." Now the look we pass among ourselves is anything but guilty.

Tamela pulls out her notebook. "Okay, I'm ready. Tell us everything you know."

~~~~~~

Hanging up, Tamela says, "Well, Hert says the Millers planned on getting on the road super early this morning. Hert and Donald went to the toy railroad exhibit up in Folkston, Georgia, last night, and he says they were totally loaded to get up before dawn and hit the road. So no getting more information from Shug unless we call her."

"This bread is delicious," Craig mumbles through his full mouth as he steps into the living room. "Oh, sorry to interrupt."

Annie beams. "I'm glad you like it. Small price to pay for letting us take over your house. We promise we'll find somewhere else to hang out now that you're around more." Innocently she adds, "Although we could turn your old bedroom into our meeting space." The sly grins tell me Craig's move upstairs has not been overlooked.

My wise husband just puts another bite of bread in his mouth and walks back into the kitchen.

Tamela clears her throat. "Hert did say they took both cars, but Donald was worried because one has a serious transmission fluid leak. The two guys had to stop and buy a supply for Donald to carry along the road to replenish it."

"Why not just get it fixed here?" Cherry says. "What's another day?"

"Oh, no," I say as I stand. "Shug was already irritated they weren't getting on the road Monday due to this railroad show. But driving both cars? That seems excessive, but maybe it's too long to be together. Shug *would* be hard to stomach on a long drive."

Annie begins cleaning up the bread. She'd left it out for Craig, but she's ready to go now. "I was up way too late last night, and now I'll barely have time to get home and change before we have to be at our Wednesday lunch. If this wasn't the last lunch of the year and reservations had to be made, I wouldn't be going."

Lucy gives her a hard stare. "But you

*are* going. I'm already going to have at least a couple cancellations, and you know they don't like cancellations this time of year at the resort."

Marisol gasps. "Was Galena Bellington in the lunch group?"

"No," Lucy responds. "But her mother-in-law, Charlotte, is, and I'm sure she's not coming. Then there's a couple ladies that have texted me they're sick. They probably just want to go shopping."

Tamela shakes her head. "Charlotte *is* coming. I called her this morning to check on her. She said some ugly things about Galena and then got mad when I insinuated she might not be coming to lunch."

I can't help but shudder. Charlotte Bellington is just downright scary. And mean. So I guess that brings the meanness out in me. "Honestly, I'm not surprised she's coming. She probably thinks we'll pay for her lunch."

But I quickly add, "Bless her heart."

I'm learning.

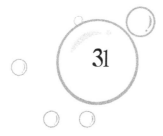

# 31

"It's real gingerbread? I had no idea when we walked past it." I look back over my shoulder, but the lobby is several halls, designer shops, and large glass doors behind us. I've never been in any of the resort restaurants. The whole place is intimidating, but everyone has been so nice and welcoming. It's grand and beautiful, from the landscaped entrance where we left our cars for the valets to take care of to the giant bouquets of flowers placed everywhere, to the shiny parquet floors and magnificent light fixtures, all directing our views to the expanse of lawn and ocean out the floor-to-ceiling windows to the rear. All that is why I neglected to realize the giant pirate ship in the lobby is made of gingerbread. I thought it was cardboard and wood made to look like gingerbread. Although, now that I think about it, it did smell more like a kitchen than a luxury hotel.

Cherry is seated beside me. "You can bring the grandkids to see it. They do some really fun children's activities over the holidays. Of course I think the spots go to hotel guests first, but I believe they're open to everyone. I'm having a glass of champagne with lunch today," she announces as she scans her menu.

Tamela and Charlotte are seated across from us. Lucy, Annie, and Marisol are also at our table for eight, which leaves one empty spot. Those three, however, are not at the table as they are in the restroom, watching the video Galena left. I'm struggling with whether I want to see it. Apparently Sergeant Johnson has released it so as to put an end to all speculation that this was anything but some unbalanced woman. Yes, he actually said that. In the news conference. Honestly, that feels even more disrespectful than watching the video.

But I just don't know.

Lucy hurries past our table to talk to the waiter who is dealing with all of us today. As she passes, she gives us a sad glance. There are four tables of eight mak-

ing up our group, so she's got a lot of organizing and communicating to do. Annie
and Marisol look sad, too, even a bit sick,
as they sit down. Annie says, "Probably
should've waited until after our lunch to
watch it."

Charlotte speaks up. "Are you talking
about my daughter-in-law's video? How
disgraceful for her to do something like
that. But it's not surprising. A desperate,
last-ditch effort for attention. Jewel, have
you seen it?"

We're all shocked at how blithely she's
acting. Except I don't think she's acting.
She's cold.

"No. I've not seen it, and I'm not sure
I will."

Charlotte pierces me with her gaze.
"You should. I want your opinion on it. I
want to see if you hear what I heard."

"What?" I squint at her. "What are you
talking about?"

The older woman flings a hand in
Marisol's direction. "You. You have it,
right? Show it to her. Now!"

Marisol looks at me, and I close my
eyes. Then I nod. "Okay, Charlotte, what
do you want me to listen for?"

"Just go. Just listen and think." She

curls a lip at me. "You can do that, can't you? Listen and think?"

"Fine. Let's go," I spit, and Marisol has to hurry to catch up with me.

When she does, she grabs my arm. "She's right. There is something, but I don't know what it is. A couple things she says are weird. Not like 'faked video' weird, but the wording. Do you think her mother-in-law thinks she's sending a message?"

"Her mother-in-law couldn't stand Galena. Can't even stand her own son because they live in the big house and turned it into an inn, which they probably did so they wouldn't lose the whole house and property, but that much reason would be beyond her. Mostly, Charlotte is just a mean old woman. I'll watch it just to get her off my back and because I won't be able to rest until I see what everyone else has seen."

Marisol's face is grim. "Daniel is appalled it was released, but apparently Frank gave Sergeant Johnson full permission. He even said he'd shared it with some people already. Galena sent the original to his phone, so I guess he had the right to do it. But yuck." She pulls me to one side once we're out in the wide hallway. "Here. This family bathroom is more private."

The small family bathroom has a couch, a vanity, and a live flower arrangement. We lock the door and sit together on the small, gold couch.

"It doesn't last very long. Here. You hold it," she says, handing me her phone.

In the video, Galena looks into the phone. Then she looks down like she's reading something. She doesn't look distraught, more like she's in a hurry. I guess if you've decided to kill yourself, you don't want to give yourself time to change your mind.

"I want to make a confession to doing all the pranks," she says. "It was all me. Not Fiona or anyone else. I was trying to impress someone who has no interest in being impressed. But that's all on me. As for Jasmine, she, uh—" Here she looks down again. Then, looking at the camera, she stumbles over her words, hemming and hawing. "You know, she knew and, uh, was following me. It was an accident, and, well, I'm sorry I left her there." Suddenly her speaking speeds up, and she focuses on the camera. "At first it was fun, but the pranking made me feel like the walls were closing in. Like there were people looking at me all the time. But small towns and old houses are like that, I guess." After a little pause, she takes on a defiant look. "I wish I could say there are people here I will miss, but after recent days I've realized there's no one here for me to miss." Then the video ends.

After taking a breath, I hand Marisol her phone back. "Okay, that's got to rip Frank and Fiona's hearts out. She won't miss them? She went with Fiona to see Charlie in prison just the other day. What in the world could've happened?"

Marisol shakes her head. "Did you pick up whatever Charlotte was talking about?"

"No. She probably just wants to point out that Galena had no friends here." I unbend from the low couch. "Let's go enjoy lunch, if that's possible. It doesn't feel like an airtight confession, but I guess that's not for us to decide."

"Well..." Marisol says with a smile. "It's kind of what we do, right?" She hugs me from the side as I tug on the shiny, brass handle. "Thank you for being my friend and introducing me to the others. It's definitely made the move easier."

The waiter is taking orders when we

return, and once that is done, the talk revolves around the upcoming holidays and anything besides murder, suicide, or the police. Apparently Lucy made that official decree while we were gone.

That's why she's our leader.

"It really is gingerbread!" I exclaim again. We took a group picture in front of the huge ship in the lobby, and now I'm reading aloud the information about it. "Three thousand eggs, thirteen gallons of milk, nine hundred pounds of sugar, and twelve hundred pounds of flour. I can't believe I didn't know about this."

Tamela sidles up beside me and whispers in my ear, "Charlotte wants a word with you over there by the windows before you leave."

I roll my eyes at her but nod. "Okay, but I rode with Annie, Marisol, and Cherry, so we're all coming."

"Oh, of course. I'll tell Lucy, too," Tamela says as she hurries away. Most of our large group has headed out to the valet station, but I motion for those I rode with to follow me. At the back of the lobby, heading out to the expansive walkways and firepits overlooking the ocean, are lots of little sitting areas and tables. Charlotte is holding one such table down, so we make straight for her.

"So, Miss Jewel," she says as we walk up. "Did you hear it?"

I shake my head. "I watched the video, and I've been thinking about it, but other than the fact that I don't feel she actually confessed to killing Jasmine, I don't know what you wanted me to hear."

Her head drops an inch or so, and she looks up at me from under heavy eyelids and bushy brows. "The walls? You did hear her mention the walls?"

"She said the walls were closing in on her."

"Then she followed that up with the fact that she felt like people were watching her all the time."

I open my mouth, but nothing comes out. Something is pinging in my head. Charlotte smiles at me and slightly nods. I find the words. "The walls in the Bellington Manor that we were behind, watching her and Frank and Fiona. You think she was talking about that for some reason?"

The others have gone completely silent. Except for Marisol they all remember how

Charlotte showed me the old hallway in her old home, where her son and daughter-in-law lived and ran the inn. How she and I snuck in there and heard lots of secret information back when I first moved to Sophia Island.

Then Annie speaks up. "They sealed that up, right? Nailed the outside door shut and even blocked the little opening into the laundry room. It's not like Galena's missing and could be hiding there."

"Then why did she mention it?" Charlotte demands. She looks around the group and can see we know she's on to something.

I pat Annie's knee. "Call Aiden. Have him meet us at the back of Bellington Manor Inn and tell him to bring a crow bar."

She jumps up and walks away as she's dialing her phone.

I turn to Marisol. "We'll explain all this on the way, but can you have Daniel figure out some way to get Frank out of his house in twenty minutes? Maybe he needs to sign something at the station or…"

She also rises. "No worries. He'll think of something."

"Charlotte, you're right," I say. "She

was sending a message. I don't know what, but there's something in that space behind the wall. And we're going to find it."

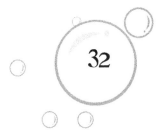

# 32

"Where's Frank?" I exclaim when Detective Ruiz comes loping around into the back garden of the Bellington Manor Inn. I had hurried over to see who was noisily coming around the side of the huge house, leaving the other women huddled next to Aiden and the small door that had been nailed shut when we got here.

"I left him in the able hands of Ms. Jones. Naomi promised not to let him out of her sight, but she says you owe her coffee at your house. I felt it was important I was here."

I wince. "Naomi. I already owe her coffee at my house. We never did get together, and we really hit it off." She's the administrator at the station and someone

I'd really like to get to know. I walk toward the house. "We're over here."

He comes closer to me as we walk and whispers, "Do I get to meet Frank's mother?"

"Scared?" I ask with a grin.

"Kind of. I hear she's a terror."

"There she is. Of course she's the first in line to get inside. But then she is the one that put it all together." Charlotte has on a red sweater, which is unusual for her usually downplayed, frumpy clothing. Dusty rose is the brightest thing I'd seen her wear until today. Then I survey our group. Greens, reds, a splash of sequins and velvet. We all look pretty festive.

Especially to be breaking into a house.

Marisol steps toward us, takes her husband's hand, and leads him to Charlotte. "Mrs. Bellington, this is my husband, Detective Daniel Ruiz."

Charlotte gives him her skeptical, one-eyebrow-raised examination, then releases a harrumph. "You've got to be an improvement over Charlie Greyson. At the very least you didn't marry a cheating liar of a woman. Can you get your boy here to move a little faster? I'm an old woman and ready for a nap."

Aiden smiles sweetly at his detractor. "The door is open. I was just stepping back to allow you to go in first. Unless you'd prefer I take on the cobwebs?"

"Of course you're to do that. But don't touch anything you see. We'll do the discovering!"

Daniel gives Aiden the high sign to proceed, then motions Charlotte and Tamela to step inside. He then mutters under his breath, "I got a search warrant just in case. I know this is Charlotte's family home, but she's no longer the sole owner."

Lucy winks at him. "Good thinking. Frank Bellington is not the understanding sort."

The dark, dusty hallway is along the end of the house. After stepping up three old stone steps, we can see the laundry room, then the kitchen through slits in the paneled wall that makes the long, narrow hiding spot. There apparently is no use for this space except for spying, and knowing Charlotte, if her parents were as suspicious as she is, that could've been exactly why it was left like this. It's not been finished or updated like the rest of the house, and just being in it again gives me the creeps. Last time I was in here I was alone, it was nighttime, and I almost was killed because of it. That's why I'm at the rear of this little expedition.

Farther along, slits in the paneling show glimpses of the living room, but only if you step right up to the wall and peer through. Cherry and Tamela have their phone flashlights on while Aiden is using a powerful police flashlight. The rest of us can see well from their lights, and we're scouring the dirty, uneven floor. Then Charlotte exclaims, "There! Pick it up, Tamela. Give it to me."

"How about Officer Bryant picks it up with his gloves, and how about we put it here in this evidence bag?" Daniel says as those two things are happening.

I hear Charlotte huff at him, but that's all she has a chance to say before Cherry exclaims, "There are pieces of paper with writing on them! There and there." Aiden moves around, picking them up and putting them in more bags that Daniel is pulling from his pockets.

"There's another one here against this wall. It's folded up," Annie says. "I've got to get out of here. This is too confining. I'll see y'all outside." She hustles past everyone, and before long, I follow her out.

In a matter of minutes we're all outside, sitting at a concrete patio table in the
pretty courtyard area. The pieces of paper
are encased in plastic but lying on the table for us all to read while Daniel is on his
phone a few steps away. He's never let the
evidence out of his sight, but he also hasn't
told us to stay away from it. I'm liking him
more and more.

We are bent over the evidence. One
bag doesn't have paper in it. "It's a thumb
drive," Cherry whispers. "Maybe the one
Shug said Jasmine had?"

"It's got to be," I say. "Except 'Bellington' is written on it."

Tamela gasps, and her dark eyes are
large as she looks up at us. "This note says
Galena didn't know Jasmine was dead, but
the thumb drive was in her bra when she
went over to look at her. She saw the name
and took it."

"She thought it was about the pranks,"
Annie reads from another slip of paper.
Then looking up to make sure Daniel
wasn't looking, she manipulates the plastic bag to unfold the paper further. "She
didn't know Jasmine was dead until the
next day! Why didn't she just tell you all

this when she came to your house? Why would she leave notes like this?"

I shake my head and think back to how she acted. "Could this be like leaving evidence in a sealed file to be found after she was gone?"

The bigger paper that was folded more than once is closest to Marisol and Annie, and they're trying to read it. The rest of us are trying to make sense of other scraps, some of which make no sense at all. "This says she's ready to get out of here, but before…" Annie huffs. "I can't read it. But 'ready to get out of here' doesn't sound like she wanted to die."

"Three million." Lucy shrugs. "This one definitely says something about three million. Dollars, maybe?"

Charlotte is sitting on the concrete bench between Tamela and me. She's silent with her eyes closed, but she doesn't look like she's asleep. I ask her quietly, "Are you okay?"

The old woman sighs heavily. "She told me goodbye. She was leaving, not planning to die."

"Who? Galena?" I ask, and I see that Marisol has gotten her husband's attention so that he can listen in.

"Yes. I did not care for her, and she did not care for me, but that plant over there by the back step is from her mother's funeral. She came to my house and asked me to take care of it. Left me some special plant food. Said she was 'going away.'"

"She wasn't planning on dying?" I ask quietly.

"No. Three million. She said she had enough to go away and never come back." She slowly opens her eyes and looks around till her eyes meet Daniel's. "Detective, I don't believe my daughter-in-law killed herself." She shuffles around on the seat. "I'm going inside. Tamela, get my walker." We all move around to help her get up. The whole time she brushes off Daniel's questions. As she and Tamela slowly maneuver down the old bricks, the rest of us sit back down; then Charlotte raises her voice. "And I'll go ahead and tell you now, detective: My son and Fiona Greyson are having an affair. I thought that was why his wife was leaving. But who knows anything now?"

Charlotte Bellington refused to say anything more. She finally told Daniel he could come talk to her at five o'clock and to bring his wife and some cake. She then shooed Tamela's help away, saying she wasn't "*that* old."

Daniel agreed to come back. He then collected all the evidence bags from the hiding place behind the wall. "I'm going to be holding Frank Bellington until I can get a look at this thumb drive. We'll be back to examine the house more closely later. Sergeant Johnson can't ignore all this."

Annie scoffs. "Don't bet on it. He's can be pretty obtuse when he wants."

We follow Daniel and Aiden out through the back gate and continue on toward my house on the next block. We parked there after lunch and walked up the street.

Tamela giggles. "We look like we're headed to a Christmas party. We're probably the most festive detectives around!"

We laugh as we stroll, but the joy quickly fades.

Lucy asks, "So, do we think Frank killed her?"

"No! I just don't want to think that," Annie says. "Especially not over someone like Fiona."

I add, "But look at Charlie. She has some kind of power over men. Besides, we need to wait and find out what's on the thumb drive."

Lucy stops at her car. "I'm not coming in. I want to check in on Mother before I go back to work." She laughs. "Back to work? I've not even been to work today! This is just a crazy time of year. Not to mention all this other stuff." We stand around and chat with her, and she shares her concerns for Birdie. All of us having just seen her, we can attest to her slowdown. Most of us had to deal with it with our own parents, and we know there's really not a lot we can do but be here for her and listen.

Tamela leans in and pulls her phone out of the car. "In all the excitement of dropping Charlotte off, then parking at your house, I forgot my phone here." She scrolls through it, then looks at me. "Hert wants to know where Craig is."

"Yeah," I say. "Hert texted me earlier and asked if I knew where he was. I told him I didn't know but would text him, but now that you mention it, Craig never responded. Let me look inside."

I run up the front stairs, open the front door, and check inside, but the house is empty. I dial Craig again, listening to the ringing while I come down the porch steps. "He's not here, and he's not answering."

Tamela holds up her phone. "Hert's not answering either. Let me locate his phone."

She pushes some more buttons, then looks up, confused. "He's at Shug Miller's house. I recognize the address, and he was there last night after the train show. It's showing him there again."

"I don't think I can do that to Craig's phone, can I?"

Annie takes my phone and examines it. "Nope. What's Hert doing out there? You said they left early, heading north."

Just then a police car screeches around the corner and bounces into our driveway.

Aiden jumps out. "Where's Craig?" he asks, breathless.

"We don't know! Why?" I ask, hurrying over to him.

"He called and left me a message about Donald Miller. Something about transmission fluid?"

"Why would he call you?"

"I don't know, but he said he's looking

into it and would let me know. I'm just hoping he didn't go out to the Millers'."

"Why?" Aiden's mom steps forward. "Shug and Donald aren't there. They left this morning."

He licks his bottom lip, and I can see his anxiety building. "I haven't seen it, but Ruiz says the thumb drive is disgusting, and along with Frank Bellington, another name jumped out at him—Donald Miller."

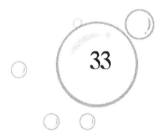

## 33

"Donald Miller is headed in his car to Rhode Island," Tamela says. "They left this morning. Hert actually talked to him just a bit ago." She carries her phone over to Aiden. "See? One of his texts says he called Donald and they were on the road." She scrunches up her nose as she reads his text. "I'm not sure what he's saying about telling Craig about coastal, um, cleanup?"

She looks at me. "Did he rope Craig into one of his projects to do some kind of cleaning at the beach?"

"Not that I know of, and I don't see anything in Craig's texts to me about him going anywhere."

Annie, who's looking over Tamela's shoulder, suddenly shouts, "Coast is clear! That's what Hert was saying. I have six kids and a couple grandkids with phones; I'm an expert at deciphering predictive text. He's telling you that he told Craig the coast is clear."

Aiden goes to his car and gets in. "I'm heading down there. Y'all just stay here and try and get a hold of the guys. I'll call Ruiz and fill him in."

Before he can back out of the driveway, Daniel pulls up and gets out of his car. We all meet beside Aiden's window. "Marisol texted me what's going on, and it doesn't make any sense. Donald Miller is one of the ringleaders, and he flew in here this morning. I was headed to his house to question him. What do you mean he was with Hert last night and is driving to Rhode Island now?"

Tamela has no answer. "That. Just that." Then she tears up. "I can't believe Hert was with someone who would hurt children. Donald has children and grandchildren of his own." Lucy puts an arm around her.

Daniel turns. "I'm getting down there. Bryant, follow me."

Of course he didn't say it, and he probably didn't mean for us to get involved this time, but of course, we're hot on his heels.

Marisol rides with Lucy, and the others are in my van.

Tamela, riding shotgun, keeps redialing Hert. "Anyone who would be involved in that kind of thing with kids wouldn't hesitate to hurt an adult. But Hert said Donald was on the road! They'd passed the South Carolina border. Maybe the guys' phones just don't work on that part of the island."

I don't look in the rearview mirror because I know my friends will be sharing looks of sympathy directed to the two of us in the front seat. I just drive, concentrating on keeping up with the police vehicles. I also don't look at the speedometer or the shocked looks of the people in the cars we're passing all the way down two-lane A1A.

At the entrance to the Millers' subdivision, I stop quickly behind Aiden, then follow him slowly as we approach the curve to the house. Two uniformed police officers meet Daniel at the end of the drive. I hurriedly park, and we are out of the car and rushing in that direction.

Daniel turns and comes to meet us. "Nothing so far. But both Craig's and Hert's cars are here."

Tamela moans, and I suck in a deep breath.

He continues. "However, we have verified the two vehicles the Millers own *are* on I-95 headed north. We didn't contact them as we didn't want to alert them, but we've had them spotted and are watching them."

Cherry has an arm around me. "But you said there's a plane ticket?"

"And an Uber from the airport to this address."

I stare at Tamela. "Children. They have children, you said."

"Which is just unconscionable," Lucy spits.

"No, no," I explain. "Donny is their son. His name is Donald Miller, and, oh my gosh! He was here this past weekend! Shug mentioned him sitting on the cream couch with his feet up watching football, and the couch wasn't delivered until last Wednesday."

Aiden slides in his car to get on his computer at the same time one of the officers near the house yells for Detective Ruiz. On top of that we hear several shouts; then all the police, including Aiden, run toward the house.

Of course, we follow.

Then we hear a gunshot.

We've stopped at the edge of the wide, paver-stone driveway, completely exposed to the cars and officers all around the house. Annie yelps and flings her arms out as if to shield us behind her. Pure cold grips me and my heart stops. There are more shouts and I wait for another gunshot. I know its coming but I can't move.

Tamela grabs at Annie to move past her and shouts, "Hert!" Then we're being rushed by a man who is shouting at us.

I finally realize it's Aiden and he's yelling, "Get in your cars. Now!"

Tamela and I both show signs we're ignoring him, but the other four ladies don't let us. We don't get all the way inside our cars, but we do stand behind my van, to the side of the road. I'm shivering uncontrollably and can't speak. Cherry is holding me tight and rubbing my arms. Tamela is sobbing quietly wrapped in Annie's strong embrace. Marisol is crouched beside the van praying. Her words are soft, but strong. Aiden is between us and the danger, his gun drawn and ready.

Then the shouting stops. Suddenly everything is so very quiet. I'm not sure I'm even breathing. The yards here are large, with dense Florida foliage. Behind the house is the golf course, so no noise comes from that direction. As a matter of fact, it's so quiet I can hear the ocean, or maybe that's just my blood racing in my ears. Tamela jerks open my car door and sits on the driver's seat with her legs hanging out. "I have to sit down. What could be happening?"

Then we hear a siren coming up behind us, and Cherry's eyes go wide. She tightens her arm around my shoulders. "Okay, I'm sure it's just a precaution, so don't be alarmed when you see it, but that's an ambulance siren."

Then the white truck with lights throbbing comes roaring by us and turns into the driveway. Marisol speaks over the blaring siren, "That is a good sign. If there was still danger, they wouldn't let it pull right up like that."

"Unless someone's dying!" I shake my head at their efforts and pull out of Cherry's grasp. "I'm going up there."

But I don't get far. Daniel comes running out of the trees straight for us, yelling, "It's okay. We got him. Miller is in custody." He keeps running toward us, then stops at me.

"But, Jewel. Craig is hurt."

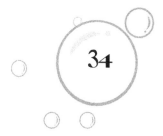

## 34

"Hert saved my life," Craig says as soon as he sees me through the open back doors of the ambulance. He's sitting up on the wheeled bed, but then I see his legs stretched out in front of him. His pants are torn or cut open, and there's blood on them.

"You want to ride with him? We're leaving now," the EMT states sharply.

"Yes!" I shout. Daniel gives me a hand up, and then I turn around. "Here are my keys." I pull them from my pocket and toss them to him.

He nods; the rest of my friends look too stunned to respond. Then the doors are shut, and I'm sitting on the end of a bench, holding on for dear life.

The EMTs don't let Craig talk, but he

gives me a big smile before they put an oxygen mask on him. They assure me he's going to be fine. The only damage is to his legs, and it doesn't look like anything too bad, but they assure me there will be a full exam at the hospital.

We arrive, and I'm quickly out the door and out of their way. I'm just going inside the emergency entrance to wait when cars race up with my chattering friends piling out of them. I turn and wait for the best huggers in the world.

I'm becoming a huge fan of hugs.

Especially the Southern variety.

We move into the waiting area, and then Cherry splits off to go over to the desk.

She comes over to where we're finding seats and says, "They'll bring the paperwork over in a bit. But everything is okay."

We all take a moment to breathe. Then I say, "Craig says Hert saved him. He couldn't talk in the ambulance. What did they tell you all?"

Tamela just shakes her head and swallows. She waves at the others to tell the story.

Annie moves closer to her and grasps one of her hands. "Hert had to go to the station to finish answering questions, but he really did save the day. Remember the whole transmission fluid leak Hert told Tamela about with the Millers' car? Well, transmission fluid is red, so when Donald Miller saw the stain beside their driveway, he decided it was just a leak from their car."

Tamela nods. "Yeah, Hert said he was there last night and saw the stain too. In the sand it looked just like transmission fluid, but he didn't really look closely. Donald told him one of the cars had been parked there all weekend." She shudders and closes her eyes.

Lucy sighs. "I guess at some point Craig got to thinking about that and wanted to check it out, so he called Hert. That's when Hert checked with Donald, who *was* on the road. Hert told Craig the coast was clear, but he was finishing up his pickleball game and couldn't go with him right then. Craig called and left messages for Aiden and Daniel, too, but they were busy with the Frank situation. So…"

"So he went to check it out himself." I shudder. "Sounds like him. Was Donny Miller already there when he got there?"

"They're pretty sure that's what happened," Cherry says. "I guess Donald told his son about the transmission fluid leak at some point when he was getting ready for the trip. Donny realized he needed to fly down here and get rid of what we assume is a bloodstain. If the car had been parked over or close to it, he may not have even realized it was there. He had a return flight for this afternoon, so it was supposed to be a quick job. He would've gotten back before his parents even got there."

"But good ol' Craig showed up." Annie reaches over to squeeze my hand with the one that's not busy squeezing Tamela's hand. The harder she squeezes, the louder she gets. "Donny hid real quick when Craig pulled up, I guess, then snuck up with a two-by-four and smacked Craig. Luckily Craig must've heard him and moved, so he only got his legs hit, not his head!"

Cherry shushes Annie. "We are in a hospital, remember." She smiles to soften her professional sternness, then looks sadly at me. "One of Craig's legs is definitely broken, but you probably could see that."

I nod. "It was pretty evident with the splints and the ways they'd had him in the ambulance. So I guess that's when Hert showed up to save the day?"

Lucy continues the story. "It is. He pulled up and saw Donny with the board, standing over Craig, looking like he was going to hit him again. Hert pulled off the driveway and aimed for Donny, who ran into the house. Hert planned on getting Craig in the car and leaving, but Craig told him Donny had gone to get a gun. He didn't think he could lift Craig in the car quick enough, so he pulled him into the shed, closed the door, and blocked it. Then they hid. He knew the police would be showing up eventually and hoped Donny would just want to get out of town or at least away from the house instead of searching for them."

"So what about the gunshot?" I ask.

"Donny." Cherry stands to take the clipboard from the woman carrying it over. "He was trying to escape out through the backyard on the other side of the house toward the golf course when an officer saw him and shouted at him to stop. Donny took a shot as he ran, but they had him down on the ground almost immediately. That's also about the time they found Hert and Craig, who were afraid to come out of hiding until they knew where Donny was."

We stare at each other for a moment, reliving those few moments that felt like a lifetime. With a tired sigh, I take the clipboard from Cherry and start filling in the blanks.

Marisol gets a text, and she exhales. "Frank Bellington is officially under arrest."

"Well, I guess you moving upstairs to Jewel's bedroom is on hold again," Annie says with a warm smile and a wink as she sits on the couch across from Craig.

Tamela frowns, admonishing her. "Be nice. And civil. Some of us are still on edge." She is seated on the hassock beside Hert's chair, and their hands are intertwined. Hert has had his fill of center stage, at least for today. He's been quiet and humble and looks like he can't believe what people are saying he did.

I'm standing behind Craig, who is in my favorite chaise lounge with his broken leg elevated. His other leg is not broken, but it is badly bruised. It was a chore getting him up the back stairs, even though we were met by everyone, ready and able to help, when we got home only fifteen minutes ago. Lucy has decreed they will all be gone in another fifteen minutes, as soon as they are sure we are in good shape for the rest of the night.

I cock my head at my nosy friend. "I'll have you know, Miss Annie, *we'll* be moving *our* bedroom downstairs for as long as needed."

I feel Craig's jerk of surprise through my hands, which lay on his shoulders. I decided in that ambulance that we are a package deal; where he goes, I go.

He lifts a hand to lay on my left hand. His speech is groggy. "Thanks, everyone, for all the help. Prognosis is good for both legs. Thank God he didn't hit my head and that Hert was there to pull me into that shed. Quick thinking, buddy."

We hear a quiet knock on the front door, which slowly opens to let Daniel Ruiz in. "I see y'all got him settled. I just wanted to stop by and fill in some of the holes. I know it'll help everyone sleep better. Uh, can I get a cup of coffee?"

Marisol jumps up. "Here, sit down. I know you have a long night ahead." She gives him a quick kiss on her way to the kitchen, and he sits in the wingback chair. We've pulled in other chairs to accommodate all six women and the five men. Ray and Martin had shown up at the hospital and came along with the parade of caretakers to help get Craig settled.

Daniel sits, then leans forward, his elbows on his knees. He gives a nod to Craig, who nods back. Then the detective clears his throat. "So this Donny Miller is a nasty piece of work. He married the daughter of one of the bosses of a crime family in Rhode Island and has steadily been on the rise. But his big contribution was financing and organizing the distribution of child pornography. I don't understand the whole business, and I don't want to, but from what the federal people have said, he streamlined it and pumped lots of money into some smaller outfits. Made a lot of money, too, for a number of people."

Marisol hands him his cup of coffee, then sits on the arm of his chair.

"Thanks, honey." He takes a sip, and we wait for him to continue. "So one of the people who made a lot of money was Joseph Ferguson—Pam, or Jasmine's, husband. From what I can figure out, Joseph had decided he wanted out, so he made that flash drive, but before he could do anything with it, he disappeared. Feds think Donny killed him or had him killed. That's when Pam disappeared, too, but she was on the run. And she had the flash drive, which she eventually brought here with her. With the time passing and her name change, she apparently thought she was safe."

"Oh no," I gasp. "I bet Shug told her son she'd run into someone from home."

"Yep. Frank says that's why Donny came down last weekend. Frank was the Florida connection with these guys. He met them at some of those meetings at the resort in the Ferguson and Miller condos where they were setting up and managing their network. Donny flew in Thursday and then surprised Jasmine at her town-house that night. He searched it but knew the flash drive could be anywhere on the island, so he took her back to his parents' home to make her talk. Speaking of his parents, they were stopped on the inter-state and are being held in Virginia to find out if they knew what was going on. Ini-tial thoughts are that they didn't. They're only guilty of believing their sweet little boy could do no wrong and of talking to him about every little thing that happened in their life—first Shug telling him about finding Pam Ferguson and then Donald spilling the beans about the transmission fluid leak."

We all take a moment to let him breathe and drink some coffee. Craig has nodded off, so we're trying to be quiet as possible and as fast as possible. Everyone is ready to leave as soon as Daniel finishes.

The detective looks tired, although his dark eyes are alert. Maybe he seems more sad than tired. Marisol rubs his back as he continues. "Frank is talking because he knows we have the flash drive, and while he likes to imagine he's some bigwig criminal, he's not. He was full of bluster this morning, but now he's petrified. Says he thinks Jasmine was killed accidentally. Not that Donny didn't plan on killing her, but it happened sooner than planned. And from the bloodstain in their yard, it did happen right out in the open, so that's probably a good bet." He looks like he's working out the crime scene in his head. "I'm wondering if he wasn't threatening her with a knife. Maybe they struggled when he was getting her out of the car and she was stabbed. Fatally. Doubt we'll ever know because Donny, unlike Frank, isn't going to talk any time soon. But he called Frank that night, told him to dispose of the body. Said Frank could move around unnoticed here better than he could and this was part and parcel of all the money he'd made. So Frank picked up the body. We have evidence from his SUV that she was in there. Then he said he thought he'd put her in your yard because he knew Galena had put the flamingos there earlier that night. In his mind, Galena would be accused of the murder *and* the pranks."

Even though we're trying to be quiet, there are several groans and incredulous expressions around the room. Annie can't restrain herself. Her eyes are blazing, but her voice is low as she says, "Then he and Fiona would be free to have the manor house and everything! And *both* spouses in jail."

Daniel smirks. "Something like that. But somehow Jasmine put the flash drive in her bra before Donny took her. That's another reason I think something went wrong with her murder; he didn't even search her. We don't know why the name Bellington was on it—maybe she was going to blackmail Frank with it—but anyway, it made Galena take it because she was afraid it contained evidence of her pranks. Apparently when she saw what was on it, she let Frank know she'd seen it. That's when he promised to give her three million dollars so she could leave the country, but she had to make the video to take all the blame off him and Fiona. He said he'd told her about the two of them and that she had no future here, but he didn't know she actually had the flash drive. He thought she'd only seen it. She wanted us to find the flash drive but only after she was gone." He shakes his head at all the insanity. "Everyone thought they could have their cake and eat it too. If she'd only just turned it in at the beginning instead of throwing it behind that wall. She'd have been embarrassed about the pranks and her husband's affair with her best friend, but at least she'd be alive."

Tamela shakes her head. "Frank was never going to let her go, was he? Not with his money. He killed her. Shot his own wife, didn't he?"

"I'm afraid so. But at least she made sure he didn't get away with everything." He moves to the edge of his chair. "I think we should let Mr. and Mrs. Mantelle go to bed." He stands and walks to the kitchen, draining his cup. Everyone else is standing and moving toward the front door when he reenters the main room. "I think that covers pretty much everything. Anything y'all can think of that can't wait until tomorrow?"

Tamela steps forward and sadly asks, "Does Charlotte know?"

He drops his head, and we hear a chuckle. "Yes. If you remember, I had an appointment to go talk to her today at five."

I put my hand to my forehead. "That was only today? It feels so long ago. But yes, after her nap she wanted to talk to you. We were at the hospital at five."

"Yes. Frank was under arrest by that time, so I went to her cottage to tell her what was going on with her son, but she wasn't there. I walked around to the front door of the big house and rang the bell because I thought I saw people through the windows. A man answered and introduced himself as the Bellington family attorney. He ushered me into the living room, where Charlotte was seated having cocktails with the inn's guests. Or, as she informed me, 'her guests.'"

He sighs and shakes his head. "She's already taken over the Bellington Manor Inn."

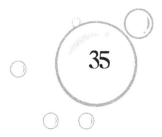

## 35

"Mom, you're buying one of these!" Andrew shouts as he flies past us, driving the rented golf cart with his father holding on for dear life on the back seat.

Our oldest, Sadie, is seated beside her brother, holding two-year-old Carver on her lap, and when I start to yell, "Slow down!", I see the joy on my grandson's face and figure his mother won't let anything happen to him. And there's nothing wrong with Craig's arms, so he should be able to hold on.

The girls, their husbands, and kids got in on time on Thursday, and Eden drove out to help me get them all home. I then traveled out to the airport to get the boys this morning. We'd waited until they got here to tell them about our latest adventure and about their dad's injuries. Renting the golf cart was Eden's idea, and she had it delivered this morning.

What will be a surprise to Andrew, who always thinks his parents have to be led kicking and screaming into new ideas, is that I already have Eden looking for a golf cart for us. For the business, you understand.

"Mom, it's so beautiful here this time of year. I never dreamed it could be so mild," Erin says. She's pushing a stroller with four-month-old Ellie in it beside me as we walk away from our house, toward downtown and the annual Dickens on Centre celebration. The orange sky above us filters through the live oak trees and moss, giving our faces a peachy glow.

Erin's husband, Paul, and Sadie's husband, Jared, are walking up ahead with our oldest son, Chris, who is discussing his future with anyone who will listen. He graduates at the end of next semester from the University of Wisconsin and can't decide what to do. Grad school or a job? The three of them are talking so intently I want to tell them to pay attention to the sky, where the winter sunset is turning everything orange.

Then I realize I'm not paying attention when Erin touches my arm. "Mom? So you and Dad?"

"Oh, sorry, honey. Yes." I turn to focus on her. "We are doing well. We're in counseling. Your dad is still going some on his own too. We have friends together for the first time that I can remember. We're actually enjoying our life here, and Dad has been enjoying doing all the things he never had time for. I don't think he's missed working at all."

"I'm excited to meet your friends. Oh, Ellie! Look at all this!"

We reach the corner and turn onto Centre Street. The marina and the sun hanging low in the sky are straight ahead of us now, but taking our attention from that beauty are hundreds, if not thousands, of white lights. The old trees are full of them, and the roof of every historic building is lined with a row of bigger bulbs. They make a dramatic ceiling to the busy street, which is only open to pedestrians for the weekend. The center of the street is full of vendor booths, and we can smell the candles, candies, and soaps as we pass. We will take our time browsing them later, but now we have friends to meet.

People dressed in period costumes walk along with those of us in jeans and tennis shoes. We slow a bit to ooh and aah at the window displays, which are decorated for a contest. Then we have to stop and examine the bookstore window, where the vintage clothing on the mannequins is made from pages of books. Every sort of edition, from children's to leather-bound, of Charles Dickens's *A Christmas Carol* is spread in front of us. There are all kinds of books associated with the famous book such as *The Man Who Invented Christmas* by Les Standiford about Dickens's writing of the book. There are even cookbooks for the foods mentioned in the classic novel. We pull ourselves away from the crowd there and continue walking down the happy street.

Up ahead, the golf cart has stopped amid a group of people where Centre Street ends at the railroad crossing. Erin points. "Is that them? Your friends?"

I see Annie and Ray, Tamela and Hert, Lucy, and Marisol at the entrance to the open platform next to the old train depot. "Yep. That's them."

By the time we reach the group, they've gotten Craig settled on a chair and places for the rest of us on the covered platform, where there are tables and chairs making up Fezziwig's Tavern. A local distillery is running the temporary "tavern" for the festival, and they sell a limited selection of drinks along with water and some nonalcoholic options.

Paul hands Erin a hot drink as he meets us at the entrance and takes over pushing the stroller. "I knew you'd want the spiked cider." He turns to me. "Craig said he wasn't sure what to order you, but I can get whatever you'd like. They've named the four drinks they offer after things in *A Christmas Carol*. I'm going to have to reread it now that they've piqued my interest."

"Then you definitely will want to stop in the bookstore. And thanks, but I'll get something in a minute. I want to introduce you to everyone."

After introductions, as everyone is chatting, I walk around to Craig and check on him. He's saved me a seat beside him, so I sit down and snuggle close to him. "How are you doing?"

"Well, if I can survive Andrew's driving, I should be able to outlast anything. You should've heard Carver laughing."

I lay my head on his shoulder, and we watch Annie making over Ellie. Erin is beaming as her daughter is enthralled with Annie's silver bangle bracelets; both girls are enthralled with Annie, as most people are. She truly is larger than life. I see Ray off to the side, and he's watching them too. I catch his eye, and he winks. I think he's going to give Annie a ring for Christmas. Okay, I don't think it—I know it! And the ring is burning a hole in his pocket.

Lucy has been pulled into Chris's deliberations over his future, and she seems to have a lot to say. Good, she gives great advice, and maybe he'll run out of steam on the subject before he starts asking me for advice again.

Tamela and Sadie are in the corner, playing a game with Carver that Tamela brought him. She's ever the teacher, and she's still in waiting mode for grandkids. Hert and Andrew have walked back to the golf cart. I'm willing to bet Hert knows more about golf carts than any of the rest of us. That's just Hert, and as far as I'm concerned, he can be as boring and know-it-all as he likes from now on. He truly did save Craig's life. I bet that's what Marisol is talking about with our two sons-in-law.

The three of them look very serious, and they keep glancing in our direction. Daniel is on duty tonight with the festivities kicking off. Things aren't too busy yet, but tonight is the big laser/drone show, and I've heard it's fantastic. Apparently the crowds really swell for that.

Most of us, however, will be home long before then. Craig is already worn out from the day and the medications he's on. Carver and Ellie also won't last that long. I'm thinking I'll encourage the adult kids to come back over and see the show. Enjoy a little adult sibling time.

"I can't believe we're here," Craig whispers to me.

I shift to look at him. "Here? You mean because of your leg? Or with the kids? Or…"

"Us. Last Christmas I had no idea this was possible. We were moving, but I wasn't happy about it. Honestly, I wasn't happy about anything." He squints his eyes. "And you weren't very happy either, were you?"

"No. But I was more scared than unhappy. Scared about everything. And now?" I look around again and pat his chest. "Now that old fear seems to be gone.

Something about facing all the things I was so afraid of made them small." I shake my head. "That doesn't make sense. I was afraid of being alone, and yet I was alone. I was scared to death of leaving the kids, and yet I didn't die, and now I get along better than ever with them. I was so sure I couldn't have friends, so I just met people knowing I couldn't make friends, and now look around."

He pushes his face into my hair. "And me? What scared you about me?"

Closing my eyes, I lean in to him even more. "I was scared you were never going to be happy. So, if I was going to be happy, I couldn't stay with you."

He sighs, and I feel his chest flatten, then fill up as he breathes in. "And that's why I went to counseling. To find out how to be happy, so we could be *here*."

Tamela raises her hand and calls for our attention. "Hey, y'all! Carver has something to say." She whispers in his ear and then gives him a little shove to step into the center of our group.

He looks at me and his papa, waves, and then says in his best Tiny Tim imitation: "God bless us, everyone!"

He then runs to bury his face in his

mother's lap, but as I meet the eyes of those in our circle, clapping and laughing, we share the sentiment silently over and over. From friend to friend, brother to sister, husband to wife.

God bless us. Everyone.

Book 7 in the
Southern Beach Mysteries Series
is coming soon!

Don't miss the first 5 books in the series!

Check out all of Kay's Southern Fiction
and Mysteries at
www.KayDewShostak.com
and she loves being friends on Facebook
and Instagram with readers.

Here is the first chapter of book one in the
Chancey Southern Fiction series. Book
twelve in the series releases in 2024.

## CHAPTER 1

So how did I get stuck driving with my
daughter, the princess, during one of her
moods? Rap music, to pacify her, adds to
my sense of disbelief. Carolina Jessup, you
have lost your mind thinking this move
can work.

Rolling hills of dry, green grass and
swooping curves of blacktop lead us to

a four-way stop. Across the road, sitting caddy-corner, is the sign I found so adorable last October. When we still owned a home in the Atlanta suburbs and moving hadn't entered the picture.

"Welcome to Chancey, Georgia. Holler if you need anything!"

A scream of "Help!" jumps to my lips, but that might disturb her highness. Maybe she's asleep and won't see her new hometown's welcome.

"Holler? Who says 'holler'? Who puts it on their sign for everyone to see?"

Nope, she saw it.

With a grimace, my voice rises above Snoop Dog, or whoever is filling my car with cringe-inducing music, as we cross the highway. "Honey, it's different from home, but we'll get used to it, right? And Daddy's really happy. Don't you think he's happy?" She dismisses my question, and me, by closing her eyes and laying her head back.

I stick my tongue out at the sign as we pass. I hate small towns.

Savannah sighs and plants her feet on the dashboard, "All my friends back home want me to stay with them on weekends." Drumming manicured fingernails on the door handle of my minivan she adds, "Nobody can believe you did this to me."

Guilt causes my throat to tighten. "Honestly, Savannah, I'm having trouble believing it, too." Apparently, she's tired of my apologizing because she leans forward and turns up the radio. Rap music now pounds down Chancey's main street, but no one turns an evil eye on our small caravan. Two o'clock on a Sunday afternoon, there's no one to notice our arrival. July heat has driven everyone off the front porches, into air conditioned living rooms. Bikes and skateboards lie discarded in several yards, owners abandoning them for less strenuous activity, like fudgesicles and Uno.

Jackson is driving the rental truck ahead of my van in which our twenty years of life together are packed tighter than the traffic at home. Oh, yeah, Atlanta isn't home anymore. As the truck takes a curve, I have a view inside the cab. With their grins and high fives, they might as well be sitting on the driving seat of a Conestoga wagon headed into the Wild West. Next to Jackson in the truck is our thirteen-year-old, Bryan. Beside the passenger window is our older son, Will. Bryan is ecstatic about this move. Will just wants to get it done so he can get back to his apartment at the University of Georgia.

We slow to take a turn where two little boys in faded jeans lean against the stop sign post. After Jackson passes, the taller one steps toward the road and waves. I press the brake pedal harder and roll down the window. Humidity and the buzz of bugs from the weeds in the roadside ditch roll in.

"Hey guys."

"You moving here?" He punctuates his question with a toss of his head toward the moving truck lumbering on down the road ahead of us.

"Sure are. I'm Carolina and this is Savannah."

The smaller boy twists the front of his red-clay-stained t-shirt in his hands and steps closer. "Ask 'em."

"I am," the speaker for the pair growls as he shoves his hand out to maintain his distance from the younger boy. "You moving up to the house by the bridge?"

"The train bridge?"

He nods and both boys' eyes grow larger. They lean toward me.

"Yes, you can come visit when we get settled."

Both boys shake their heads and the designated speaker drawls, "No, ma'am. Can't." He pulls a ball cap out of his back pocket and tips his head down to put it on.

The little one keeps shaking his head and finally asks, "Ain't you afraid?"

Savannah moans beside me, "Mom..."

"No, we like trains. Well, we'd better be going."

"You ain't afraid of the ghost?"

My foot jumps off the accelerator and finds the brake pedal. My finger leaves off rolling up my window. "What?"

But they don't hear me. The boys are running toward the house sitting in the yard full of weeds.

Savannah grins for the first time today. "Did he say 'ghost'? Cool." She turns the music back up, lays her head against the head-rest and we pull away from the corner.

*Ghost? Like there's not enough to worry about.*

Tiny yards of sunbaked grass and red dirt pass on the left. Across from them a string of small concrete buildings house a laundromat, a fabric store, and Jeans-R-Us. Chancey's version of an open-air shopping mall. Hopefully, Savannah's eyes are closed as I speed up to catch the truck. Over a small hill, the truck comes into view along with a railroad crossing. A smile pushes through my worries as I think of the grin surely on my husband's face right now.

For years, Jackson talked about moving and opening a bed & breakfast for railroad enthusiasts, railfans, in some little town. Now, a lot of people fantasize about living in a small town. I believe those are the people who have never lived in one—like my husband.

Only five weeks ago, he came home with a job offer from the railroad. We'd already experienced life with the railroad in our early married life. When we finally tired of his constant traveling, he took a job with an engineering consultant and we moved to the upscale suburbs northwest of Atlanta. Railroad job, or no, nothing was getting me out of the suburbs.

Then I find condoms in Savannah's purse, freak out, and accidentally make his dream come true. Well, the small town part of his dream, but the B&B is not happening. Things won't get out of hand again, not with me focusing.

At the railroad underpass there is no stop sign or light, but Jackson and the boys are stopped anyway. Arms poke out of both windows of the truck cab. There's no train coming but Bryan and Will spent more father-son outings in rail yards than parks so they could be pointing at one of a hundred things of interest.

At first Jackson's train obsession was cute, but I realize now, I'm an enabler. Like the husband walking down his basement stairs when it dawns on him his den could double as a scrap-booking store. Or the wife suddenly realizing her last ten vacations involved a NASCAR event.

Past the railroad yard and up the hill overlooking town, the harsh sunlight is muted by thick, leafy boughs drooped over the street. Shade allows for thick lawns encased behind wrought-iron fences or old-stone borders. Sidewalks cut through the lawns and lead to deep front porches and tall houses. The houses stand as a testament to Chancey's once high hopes—hopes centered on the railroad and the river. As we come to the top of the summit the River runs on our right.

Savannah leans forward to look out her window, pushing her dark hair back. Ahh, even she can't ignore the view.

"Mom, you realize we are officially in the middle of nowhere, right? Look, nothing but trees and water as far as you can see. Not even a boat in all that water. I guess everybody's inside watching *The Antiques Roadshow.*"

So much for enjoying the view. We turn away from the river and start back down the hill, taking a sharp turn to our right. A narrow road maneuvers through a green channel of head-high weeds. The road and weeds end in wide-open sky and a three-track crossing.

"Great, a stupid train already," Savannah growls. We can't see the train but up ahead her father and brothers are out of the truck and pointing down the line. We both know what that means.

I put the van into park and lay my head on the steering wheel. My sense of disbelief wars with the memory of the joy on my husband's face. Is it possible for us to be happy here? A train whistle blows as dark blue engines rock past and my head jerks up. Through the blur of rushing train cars I see the other side of the tracks—and our new home.

Frustration cuts through my sadness because someone is sitting on the front porch. Are you kidding me? A drop-in visitor already?

Find the rest of *Next Stop, Chancey* and the other Chancey books on Amazon.com or at your local bookstore.

Printed in the USA
CPSIA information can be obtained
at www.ICGtesting.com
JSHW021906011223
52991JS00001B/2